FRANKENSTEIN'S MISTRESS
Tales of Love & Monsters

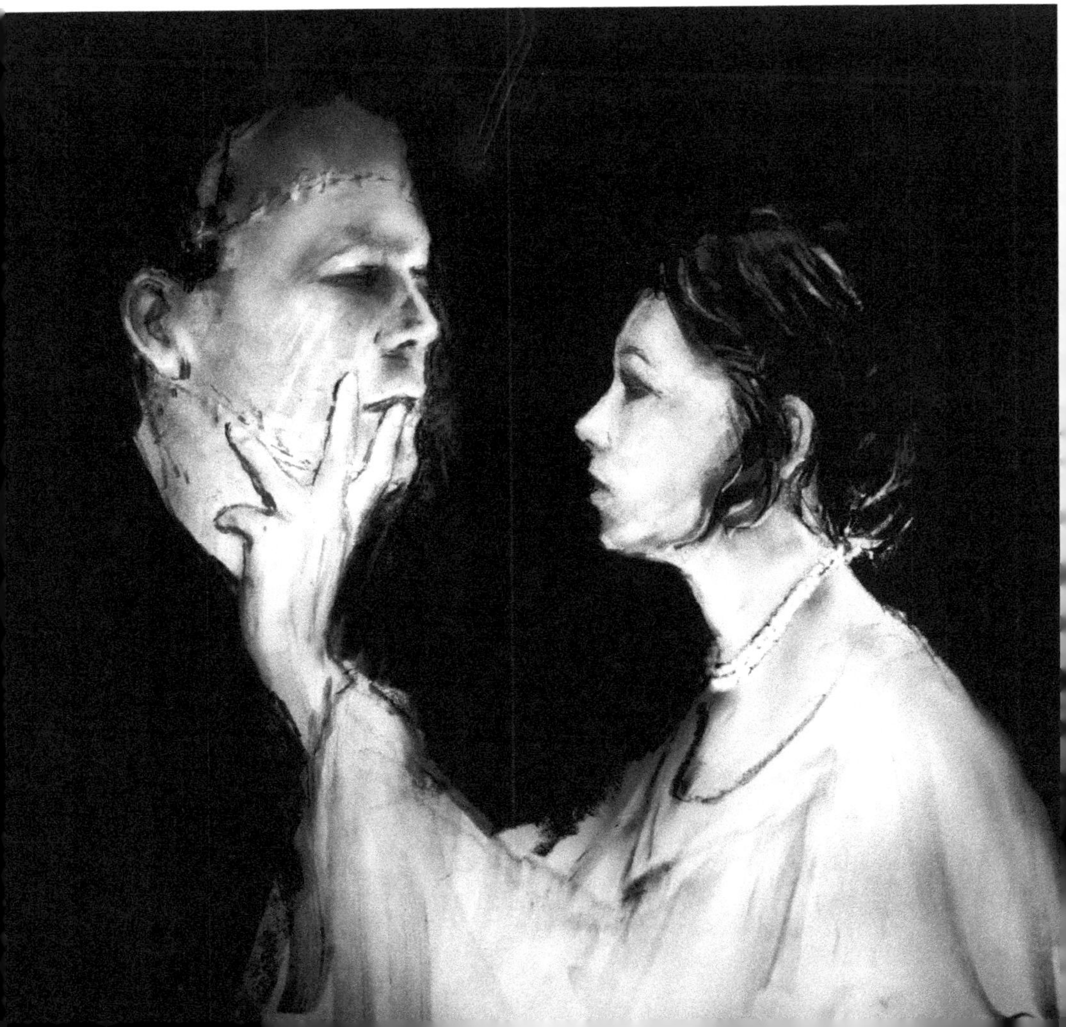

Also By Michael McCarty:

Short Story Collections:
Dark Duets by Michael McCarty (2005), Wildside Press
A Little from My Fiends by Michael McCarty (2014), Wildside Press
Dracula Transformed & Other Bloodthirsty Tales by Mark McLaughlin & Michael McCarty (2016), Wildside Press
Dark Cities: Dark Tales by Michael McCarty (2019), Amazon
Frankenstein's Mistress: Tales Of Love & Monsters by Michael McCarty (2020), Grinning Skull Press

Novellas:
Lost Girl of the Lake by Joe McKinney & Michael McCarty (2017), Grinning Skull Press

Novels:
Apocalypse America! by Michael McCarty & Mark McLaughlin (2019), Amazon
Liquid Diet & Midnight Snack by Michael McCarty (2011), Simon & Schuster
Bloodless series: *Bloodless, Bloodlust, & Bloodline* by Michael McCarty & Jody LaGreca (2012), (2013), (2016), Simon & Schuster

Non-Fiction:
Giants of the Genre by Michael McCarty (2003), Wildside Press
More Giants of the Genre Michael McCarty (2005), Wildside Press
Ghostly Tales of Route 66 by Michael McCarty & Connie Corcoran Wilson (2008), Quixote Press
Conversations with Kreskin by The Amazing Kreskin & Michael McCarty (2012), Team Kreskin
Modern Mythmakers by Michael McCarty (2013), Crystal Lake Press
Ghosts of the Quad Cities by Michael McCarty & Mark McLaughlin (2019), Haunted America

FRANKENSTEIN'S MISTRESS
Tales of Love & Monsters

Michael McCarty

(with C.L. Sherwood, Holly Zaldivar, Terrie Leigh Relf,
R.L. Fox, Cindy McCarty,
& Sherry Decker)

Introduction by C. Dean Andersson

Afterword by Cristopher DeRose

A
Grinning Skull Press
Publication

DEDICATION

Dedicated to Charlee Jacob

Also to Michael J. Evans, Harrison Graves, and the rest of the Grinning Skull Press staff; Bruce Walters; C. Dean Andersson; C.L. Sherwood; Cristopher DeRose; Holly Zaldivar; Sherry Decker; Terrie Leigh Relf; Ron Fox; Jeff Ernst; Jody LaGreca; Ray Congrove; Bonnie Lou; Brad Heden for letting me helm "Major Tom" magazine from 1982-1988; and, of course, Cindy McCarty, who will always be the lovely bride to my monster.

CONTENTS

ACKNOWLEDGMENTS

Holly Olsen, Jack William Finley, Camilla, the Hultings, the Leonards, Larry Nadolsky, William Curtis Mohr, David & Julie, Jo Ann Brown, Chef Steph, Brian Kilgore, Brian Kronfeld, the Mirons, The Book Rack, Char, The Source Bookstore, Marlena Midnite, Judy, Joan Mauch, Renée Bushā, Amber B, the memory of my parents, the memory of Kitty & Latte, The Quad City Rollers, and Joyce Godwin Grubbs.

Editors: Michael J. Evans, Harrison Graves, & C.L. Sherwood

Proofreaders: Ann Attwood, Jeff Ernst, Holly Zaldivar, & Cindy McCarty

INTRODUCTION

C. Dean Andersson

There really is a Castle Frankenstein, you know, eleven miles from the German town of Gernsheim. In the 1600s, a man performed strange alchemical experiments there. Two centuries later, a teenager passed near that castle on a journey along the Rhine on her way to Switzerland, and that night, her astral body traveled to the castle while she was asleep because a spirit from the future came to her in a dream and said, "Hi, Mary! I'm Michael McCarty! I'm creating a book of great stories called *Frankenstein's Mistress* inspired by your famous novel!" Whereupon Mary Shelley, still asleep, answered with her thoughts, "What famous novel? I have not written a famous novel. I must be dreaming." Whereupon Michael McCarty answered, "Then your dream must be that you want to write a famous novel, and I can help your dream come true! Collaborate with me! Okay? And start by coming with me tonight to a spooky castle!"

"Sir!" said Mary Shelley with her thoughts, still dreaming, "I cannot go to a castle alone with a strange man! My reputation, sir! My reputation!"

"It's just a dream, Mary, remember? No one will know, and it will make you famous. There will soon come a night when you are challenged to write a ghost story by your companions. You will write a story, if you come with me tonight, that will be known for hundreds of years and inspire countless other writers and artists over the centuries to come!"

So! Mary Shelley went with Michael McCarty, and they astral-projected to Frankenstein's Castle, where he told her a strange story of a man who created a monster by reanimating a creature he had made from the bodies of the dead, and the rest is history.

Thank you, Mary Shelley!

Thank you, Michael McCarty and C.L. Sherwood!

Classics Illustrated introduced me to Mary Shelley's *Frankenstein*. I still have that comic book. Monster Kids keep their treasures and their love of classic monsters. But many also create their own. Perhaps we have also visited Frankenstein's Castle in dreams, as well as the neighboring Castle Dracula.

Now, after years of watching Frankenstein movies and reading Frankenstein books, even writing a Frankenstein book myself called *I Am Frankenstein*, a companion to my *I Am Dracula*, I have the honor of introducing you to Michael McCarty's lovingly created tale, *Frankenstein's Mistress*.

The stories in this book are the creations of fine writers inspired by the sinister fruit of the spectral night when Michael and Mary traveled in astral form to the castle. In an alternate reality, Michael and Mary performed together in a wildly popular comedy vaudeville act.

So! This book is the product of other fine writers' dreams spawned by a dream hundreds of years ago, but at the center of it all is Michael McCarty!

Go read those stories now. Enjoy! Dream! Have fun!

A storm is rising somewhere in the world.

Thunder and lightning!

A dead hand stitched to a dead arm twitches.

It's alive!

I've wanted to write a sequel to the Frankenstein *novel since college. I had originally wanted to do the project with Joyce Godwin Grubbs, who was a distant relation to Mary Shelley (the author's maiden name was Mary Wollenstonecraft Godwin) but it never panned out.*

I found out C.L. Sherwood extensively studied Mary Shelly and the Frankenstein *novel in college and that sparked my interest in doing the project again.*

This novella is dedicated to three wonderful ladies: Mary Shelley, Joyce Godwin Grubbs, and C.L. Sherwood.

FRANKENSTEIN'S MISTRESS

C.L. Sherwood & Michael McCarty

PART I: The Captain's Tale

Chapter 1: A Tragic End

North Sea – Artic Circle

The sun beat on the ice and sea, reflecting off the surfaces like a mirror. As he ran, the creature shielded his eyes against the glare, heart pounding and aching to the point where anger and pain knew no separation. While his heart ached for his creator, he detested his creator's rejection, the stinging of his words and denials, and had wanted nothing more than the suffering to match his own. When he reached the edge of one ice sheet and another passed close enough, he vaulted across without a single thought about slipping, being crushed in a crevasse, being lost to the sea, or any other dangers. In this way, he ran from the vessel, from the captain, the sailors, his dead creator, and all who gave him such misery and all whose scared eyes hated him without knowing him. He had no sense of direction; he just followed the floating path before him, his feet pounding the ice, his mind focused.

Through that day and well into the night, he kept the pace, never daring to feel. Yet, as the sun rose the next morning, he tired and longed for peace, any peace. When he looked around and no longer saw the vessel in any direction, he gave in to his exhaustion and crumpled to the ice. Let it take him where it might; let the cold take him where it might. The creature lay on the ice, impervious to the freezing temperatures, staring at the stars, the snow falling in fits and swirls, and thought about all he'd been denied, the love he'd never know, the acceptance he'd never feel.

Chapter 2: Creator and Created

The vessel moved at a snail's pace among the ice sheets, most sails dropped. The captain stood on the forward deck in his peacoat and scarf with a spyglass in his gloved hand; the icy wind picked up and died in bursts as he searched for the creature, the monster, the miserable soul that jumped from the ship the day before. The North Sea churned but was somewhat calmer than the previous day, yet it remained active as the ice sheets broke apart with resounding cracks, creeks, and splashes. He lowered the glass, turned, and gazed at the body of his friend, Victor Frankenstein, frozen on the deck, chalky white and blue…and could not look away. Frankenstein's story had captivated him and had shaken him physically and spiritually. What was of particular interest was an account of how Victor had started the experiments when he was at the university and how he had his father, Alphonse, fund them, including buying an abandoned castle outside of Cambridge. It was a sad thing that the creation his father had funded had also inadvertently been the cause of his father's death. At first, he hadn't believed the stories about the creature Frankenstein had brought to life, thinking Victor a sad madman, deranged in some manner. He hadn't believed then that it was possible to reanimate dead flesh, but he'd seen someone large on a sled just minutes before he'd encountered the half-dead Victor talking with his crew. Over time and many conversations, he'd come to love Victor and loathe the monster he'd never met…until he did—a creature of great stature and horrific deformity. Yet, even as repulsed by the sight as he was and filled with the truth of mayhem and murder Victor relayed, he'd felt sorry for the miserable creature, who'd come across so intelligently, so emotionally, so…human. The captain returned to scanning the frozen sheets until his blood began to run with ice; his hands ached and stiffened.

Several sailors busied themselves chipping ice off the mainsails and lines, knocking it off the railings and freeing up equipment and hatches—a sea of steamy breath plumed as they worked, like a man puffing a pipe. A few sailors picked up larger chunks of ice and placed these into buckets they carried into the galley to melt by the pipe stove. Others they took to the bowels of the ship and into the storage room. On deck, the water barrels stood frozen solid and had become too heavy to move; the ice melted in the galley would provide much-needed fresh water. Two other sailors endeavored to catch fish in the growing cervices between ice sheets, and a bucket near them attested to their success.

The captain grabbed the arm of the nearest sailor, who turned to look at him with tearing but clear blue eyes, ice chunks in his cloth-wrapped, calloused hands, his nose red and running into his mustache and beard, and ice on his brows and lashes. The captain held out the glass. "Keep a steady watch for that creature. He can't have gone far."

The sailor dropped the ice chunks into the bucket and took the glass. "Aye, Capt'n," he said, walking to the railing and lifting the glass to his eye.

The captain made his way down to the galley and the warmth of the stove pipe, whereupon he poured a cup of tea from the pot on the stove and warmed his hands while he drank. Some sailors busied themselves with ever-decreasing provisions to make a fish stew for that night's dining. Fish they had plenty of, but potatoes, onions, carrots, and other vegetables had grown scarce. It'd been several months since they'd tasted any fruit, and their coal supplies were dwindling. He set the cup on the edge of the stove and headed for the deck.

As he arrived on deck, the sailor he'd given the glass to was shouting and waving, "Capt'n!"

The captain hurried over. "Did you find him?"

"Aye, Capt'n. I think so." He pointed, handing the captain the glass. "I saw a large, still form on the ice."

Taking the glass, the captain scanned the area. A large form lay close to the edge of the ice sheet, and he recognized it. The creature. The captain put down the glass and turned. "Prepare to lower the dinghy. Bring a rope and the gaff."

The captain and four sailors boarded the dinghy. As members of the crew lowered the eight-man rowboat to the sea, the captain gazed again at the still form on the ice some distance away, but his mind focused on Victor's lifeless body. Of course, he would deliver both to the proper authorities in London, and they could sort out this mess. He thought about the papers and letters, all the information imparted to him by Victor over the course of their friendship. Maybe he'd keep those, partly because they had been Victor's and partly because he worried that others would follow the same crazy endeavors as Victor had. Often, people who cringed at the ideas of raving lunatics and madmen took it upon themselves to "fix" the issues that kept the very thing they feared from working properly.

"Slow and steady," the captain said. The boat made slow progress among the shifting ice sheets until it closed in on the creature's location. One of the sailors used an oar to poke the monster, but it was like tapping the ice.

"Think it's frozen," the sailor said.

"Let's find a level plain to get onto the ice and get him on the boat," the captain said.

The temperature had begun to fall again, and the sky, which had been clear just hours ago, now loomed dark. Fear crept up the captain's spine; if the free water froze again like it had just days ago, they could be trapped, maybe permanently. He thought about the stories he'd heard of other ships that sailed these waters—those sad vessels lay ice-locked somewhere in this arctic ice plain. At least one had been discovered, along with its frozen crew, but unfortunate others like it lay undiscovered, like ghosts. As far he knew, no one from those missing ships had ever returned. He shivered. That wasn't going to be his ship *or* his crew.

The sailors rowed the boat to a reasonably even part of the shelf. Using the gaff and rope, three sailors struggled onto the ice one by one, the boat bumping against the ragged edge and rocking. The last sailor lost his footing and began to slide, his shoe lapped by the sea. The captain grabbed him by his jacket and steadied him while he regained his footing. The boat thumped into the jagged ice below the water line and steadied.

"Easy does it, boys," the captain said.

When the men were safely on the ice sheet, shivering and crossing their arms for warmth, the captain said, "Hurry now. If this ice shifts toward the boat, we're finished."

The sailors nodded and made their way like a line of polar explorers trekking against the wind to the creature's frozen body. For a moment, they all stared at the grotesque form as if mourning him, then they tugged and pulled and grunted, rocking the body back and forth to loosen it from the ice's grip. When the body gave way, sliding, the men threaded the rope under its arms and around its legs and tied it. The creature's body proved too heavy to lift, so the men pulled it along the ice toward the boat as if it were a sled and they dogs.

The captain dared not stand, but he reached with the gaff, snagging the rope around the creature's chest. "Steady, now," he said, as the men struggled to lower the body across the short distance into the boat. One of the sailors jumped from the ice into the boat to steady the body as it slipped. The small ship rocked and bumped the ice, nearly spilling them all into the sea.

"Bloody hell!" the captain yelled as he worked to steady the dinghy. "Steady, now!"

Once settled, the small boat weighted down to the point where the water rose halfway up the sides, the other two sailors boarded. The crew, squished together like sardines, managed to row the boat back to the ship, where lines were lowered; they attached the hook rings to the ropes and hoisted the body to the deck.

Once safely on deck, the captain stared at the creature's body and wished people, especially himself, hadn't treated the creature with so much hatred, but what was done was done. He couldn't undo any of it. Several sailors pulled the creature's body next to Victor's, and the captain felt an odd compassion—creator and created were together at long last. The captain gave the order for the ship to sail toward England.

Chapter 3: Changes, Secrets, & Lies

For the first few days, the captain didn't sleep well; he worried about hitting icebergs or getting ice-locked as the ship inched its way through the spreading ice sheets, amid the rough surf of the North Sea, and into warmer waters. At that point, to his great relief, the weather cleared, sailing speed increased, and they were making good time. That first week the ship sailed in calm waters, and the weather continued to improve, though it never reached above fifty-five degrees. It was colder than it had been in past years, and he'd had news that scores of people were dying due to failed crops in cities all over Europe. He welcomed the sun's warmth, however slight. The thick ice of the Arctic lay far behind, and the misery of poverty-stricken England lay ahead.

During the second week, the weather took a turn for the worse, and seas crashed against the hull. Many of the sails he'd dropped, and the few that remained were levied against the wind to keep them steady. It was slow going. In such weather, the sails could be torn from the masts and the ship left to the fate of the sea. Yet, the captain welcomed such storms, which brought fresh water that collected in empty barrels and cleaned the months of sea from the ship, its deck, and its sailors. The warmer weather began to melt the remaining ice and thaw the last of the ice-encrusted water barrels. Cold water pooled at the tops. Food supplies, however, grew scarcer with each passing day. The warmth, while welcomed by the crew and which allowed for easier sailing, worked against the remaining food supplies, especially the fish stores. The cook salted and dried what he could, but much of it had to be thrown overboard in the end. That same heat began to work on the bodies of Victor and the creature, too, so he had the sailors move them below deck into a storage room deep within the bowels of the ship, farthest from the galley, near some still-frozen water buckets, in a feeble attempt to keep the bodies gelid. The temperature remained cold, but not quite frigid. Even an old scallywag like him knew if he wanted to preserve a body, he needed to keep it frozen, not just cool.

It was there, in the bowels of the ship, that the captain sat in the last days of the journey, alternately staring at the bodies and sifting through Victor's letters and notebooks. The room was still chilly, but he could see that Victor's feet and hands had begun to blacken and that his belly had begun to swell. A stench wafted up through the decks, and though the sailors found this smell distasteful, they never complained. The creature's body, on the other hand, was still cool and looked like it did when he'd found it. They were only a few days out of port now.

At the start of the journey home, the captain had been curious more than anything else about Victor's experiments and reanimation endeavors. But now, after nearly a week of thought and reading, he found himself interested in this reanimation process, at the possibilities it implied. He'd seen the proof of its success, but more than that, he missed the friend he grown so fond of, the man with the wild and brilliant mind.

Day in and day out, the captain thought about Victor and his creation, about the authorities, about his duties, about what would be the right thing to do. He thought about Victor's crazy but brilliant ideas, poured over his notes and letters, and worked through the math equations and the science. Somehow, it all began to make sense to the captain, a strange sense that he couldn't avoid or explain. Victor accomplished what no one else had, and though he'd turned from his creature and hunted him like an animal, he'd kept all the experiment notes and a detailed account of the night he brought the creature to life. *Why had he kept these if he never intended to use them or publish them*, he wondered. The captain feared what the authorities would do if they ever found Victor's notes; he'd been so steadfast on destroying it all. Now, after weeks of thought, he found himself at the center of those fears, the reasoning behind keeping the notes from authorities. He had decided that—with the right help and the brightest minds—he might be able to reanimate the creature without having a brain that was prone to violence and criminality: Victor's brain. The brain, *whose brain*, would prove to be the "fix" to Victor's failure with the creature. In effect, he'd been wrong to judge Victor's experiment so harshly; the man had been ahead of his time.

The captain fetched an ice pick from a box and hacked at the large ice chunks still in the buckets. Icy water and tiny ice shards sprayed his face, his pace feverish. After he'd finished several buckets, his arms and hands aching, he sifted the broken ice out and put the pieces into sacks and laid these around Victor's head.

"Excuse me, Capt'n?"

The captain looked up, startled, to see a sailor holding a tray.

"You've been down here for days. The men thought you might be hungry," the sailor said.

"Thank you. Just set the tray on the barrel next to me."

"Aye, Capt'n. Can I get you anything else?"

"No. I'm quite fine as I am," the captain said without looking up.

The sailor turned and left.

When the captain heard the door at the top of the stairs close, he eyed the tray. A square of bread nestled next to a bit of fish on a spot of rice with a small piece of potato and carrot. He realized this was more than the sailors fed themselves. He wished he hadn't been so dismissive to the sailor delivering his meal. His stomach growled, and he felt the saliva thicken in his mouth, so he ate despite his guilt and sipped the tea while reading the notebooks again. He had a good idea of what needed to happen when they reached port but wasn't sure how to get the bodies off the boat to a cool and safe place. He fell asleep thinking about it.

The next morning, the stench of Victor's body was almost unbearable. That was when the idea came. He only needed Victor's brain. He would remove Victor's head and pack it in the remaining ice. That seemed the right way to go since Victor's head was still frozen…mostly. He looked around the space. The crate he sat on was too big for the head and too small for the creature. The long, wide pallets stacked against the wall caught his eye. Aye, those would do the job. Old blankets sat folded in a crate. He'd just wrap the creature and tie him to a pallet and mark it as his personal property. He discovered a smaller crate, too, which was perfect for Victor's head. The captain tied a bandana around his face and commenced his gruesome deeds.

By early evening, the captain's plans were well underway. He'd retrieved the ax from the galley and emptied the small wooden crate. He opened the box and lined it with the large leaves they used for smoking fish. Picking up the ax, he turned to Victor's body. Heaving the ax, it hung above his head for few lingering moments, and then he swung, his aim true. Pink and red ice shards flew, like small explosions, and clung to ax's edges. Other than that, hacking off Victor's mostly frozen head proved relatively easy and far less messy than he'd imagined.

With tenderness, he packed Victor's head inside the crate, closed it, marked it as his personal property, and set it aside. Afterward, as he rolled Victor's decomposing body onto some cloth, a wheezing noise followed by a foul stench stopped the captain in his tracks. Victor's abdomen tore open and fell apart like overdone mutton, spilling watery, slimy, half-formed entrails on to the cloth. The captain reeled, retching and coughing. Breathing heavy and sweating, the captain composed himself enough to finish the job. The spilled entrails and fluids hadn't reached the floorboards, though blood soaked the cloth; nothing a good swabbing wouldn't take care of.

The creature, much heavier and larger, proved more challenging to deal with. The captain managed to wrap his body in several blankets and tie it up with rope. Once he lugged it onto the pallet, he tied the creature in place and sandwiched it between several empty crates with another pallet on top, then tied those together. He stepped back to judge his handiwork. *It really didn't look like a body*, he thought, and he found he was pleased with these results, which only weeks ago would have repulsed him. Such was the human condition, constantly changing and shifting.

The captain dragged Victor's wrapped body onto another pallet and tied it down. Huffing and wheezing, he hauled it like a sled up the stairs and onto the deck.

"Come, boys," the captain said, panting. "Let's give my friend, Victor Frankenstein—a man who spent years at sea exploring life's possibilities—a seaman's burial."

Several sailors picked up the pallet like a casket and attached it to the rigging. They lowered it to the sea.

The captain looked down as one sailor shimmied down the line and unhitched the ropes. "Any words, Capt'n?"

The captain took a deep breath and stepped forward. "Victor was a brilliant man, misunderstood by most. May he find the peace he so richly deserves," he said, nodding for the men to release the body, though he knew this wasn't the end of Victor Frankenstein.

The sailor pushed the pallet away with his foot and shimmied back up the rope to the deck. All watched the pallet toss in the white-caps and sink into the sea. Relief washed over the faces of the crew; the captain felt it, too, a kind of release. All he needed to do now was gather Victor's notes and letters, and all would be ready for port when they landed in the morning.

By the time the captain had gathered his personal effects into his sea bags, it was evening. He headed for the deck and the last night of this expedition. In the distance, he could see the lights of the Port of London.

Chapter 4: Packing Up Sanity

London, England: Port of England

The ship arrived in London's harbor early the next day, and the captain stood watching by his readied cart, stroking the horse's neck, as the cargo made its way to shore on the backs of his sailors. When he saw his belongings come down the plank and the sailors carrying them make their way toward him, the captain's heart leaped into his throat, and he thought his heart might burst from his chest. A sailor held the crate containing Victor's head. He feared the ice melting inside might leak.

"Mornin', Capt'n," the sailor said. "Where do you want this trinket, then?"

"Thank you," the captain said, taking the box with care. "I'll take it from here." He found it a home on the floorboard by the driver's seat and covered it with the blanket waiting there.

"And these, Capt'n?" asked another sailor toting two sea bags.

"Just in the back is fine. Thank you," he said.

A few agonizing minutes lapsed as he waited for the pallet with the creature's body. He thought he must be a raving lunatic for doing this thing he was planning; yet, he was excited, too. Wasn't he? Aye, almost giddy. Was this the way Victor felt? It must have been, and now he could clearly understand the obsession. Soon, the deceased Frankenstein would be resurrected. Together, there would be no limits to their possible achievements.

Six sailors dragged the captain's pallet down the debarking ramp, and two others steadied the cargo. Once off the ramp, the men were able to pull the pallet to where the captain awaited.

"On the back, then, Capt'n?" asked a sailor.

"Indeed. And be careful. The contents are fragile."

Almost at once, the sailors said, "Aye, Capt'n." They looked at one another with questioning eyes but did as instructed.

"Cover that with the blankets and tie it down," the captain said.

"Aye, Capt'n," the sailors replied.

"Good lads."

By late afternoon, the ship was emptied and the cleaning and repairing had begun. As the sailors filed by the captain and he paid them their wages, he thought of the castle Victor had told him about. No one knew Victor was dead.

When he'd completed his task, he walked over to the harbormaster. "Excuse me," he said, tapping the man's shoulder. "I've been at sea for quite some time on an expedition. Last news I heard from London was that a monster fled Victor Frankenstein's castle. Anything new on that front?"

The harbormaster smiled, his round red cheeks pushing his too blue eyes almost closed and making his graying handlebar mustache curl close to his nostrils. "Yeah, and plenty," he said, appearing cheerful for interaction other than harbor business. "The constables searched the castle, the land, the woods, and the surrounding countryside for months, but they ain't never found nothing." He shook his head. "You'd think the authorities could find something as big as that, now, don't you?" His smile faded. "They are still looking, I hear. They questioned Frankenstein, but he couldn't tell them anything about the monster other than to drip with obvious hatred for the creature."

"Well, that is news, and the latter would not at all surprise me since the creature killed his family. Do you know the whereabouts of Frankenstein's castle or whether or not it is still guarded?" the captain asked.

"No. Sadly, Frankenstein left for an expedition shortly after he buried his fiancé. He hasn't come back that I'm aware of. You might ask at the pub or the university. The castle—quite a marvelous piece of work—is abandoned since Frankenstein left, I'm afraid. It appears he let go any help he had before he left. It's been months now. No one goes up there anymore, from what I hear."

"Well, that's a shame. He invited me to the castle whenever I came into port. I suppose I could check in on the place, tidy things up a bit," the captain said. "And thank you."

The harbormaster smiled and nodded.

The captain knew the harbormaster to be a talker, and news of his occupation of the castle would spread; he would be considered welcome, would keep the grounds, and await the owner's return. He headed in the direction of the countryside on the outskirts of London and Victor's castle.

Chapter 5: Somewhere Safe…

As the cart made its way around the curving road, headed uphill to green fields and rocky inclines, the captain caught his first glimpse of the large stone castle just as the sun fell below the horizon in splashes of red, orange, and smears of dark gray and purple. Sprawled across the hilltop, it had several sections, with the middle section being taller than either of the ends. *The only things missing*, the captain thought, *were a moat and a drawbridge.*

"Whoa. Whoa," the captain said, pulling on the reins. He sat for a moment in awe, looking up. Then he climbed down from the cart, picked up the lantern, and lit it. Following the path to the porch, he made his way to the larger-than-life doors. He didn't know why, but he knocked and waited, then knocked again. When no one came, he pushed the door open and stepped across the threshold.

Cold and drafty, the entry was nearly barren of furnishings. A large, round rug was centered on the floor near a stone staircase that wound its way up into the darkness. "Hello?" the captain called out, the sound echoing. No one responded.

From room to room, the furnishings sparse and covered in plain white sheets, the captain walked, stopping now and again to admire a tapestry or painting, until he found the ornate door Victor described during their conversations. He pulled on the doorknob. Locked. He knocked on the wood with the back of his knuckles—a thick *thump thump thump*. Solid wood. Pulling a notebook from his jacket pocket, the captain remembered reading about the keys or a key ring. He thumbed through the carefully scripted, yellowed, dog-eared pages until he found the passage. He tapped the page and closed the notebook.

Working his way back through the hallways, he found the kitchen. By the pantry door, a ring of keys hung from an iron hook on the wall. *Which key, though?* He gazed at several of them. They weren't marked, but that didn't matter. He'd try them all, if need be. He returned to the ornate door.

The first ten keys didn't fit, but on the eleventh attempt, he heard the loud click of the lock releasing. He marked the key with a scrap of cloth and put them in his jacket pocket. Pushing the door open, he could see just the top of the steep, winding stone stairwell that disappeared deep into the room below. He looked along the walls for a way to light the room; he found nothing. Without a railing, the captain made his way down the stairs, one hand guiding him along the wall, the other holding his lantern.

At the bottom, he held the lantern high and tried to get a feel for the room; the light's circle, however, was too small and diffuse to see well enough. The space was large, and he could feel a draft much stronger here than he had upstairs. He moved toward where he thought a wall might be and found contraptions of the sort he'd seen drawn into Victor's notebooks. This was indeed Victor's lab, dusty from disuse, as it might be. In the center of the room, a large table framed by levers had been locked onto a platform; chains led from the table up into the darkness. From this vantage point, he could see the stars of the night sky and realized there must be a large opening in the roof. He moved back to the stairs.

As captivated by this discovery as he was, the captain knew needed to get his belongings inside while it was dark just in case this place wasn't as isolated as he'd first thought. He'd figure all the rest out in the morning, when he could see how things were and how they worked.

Back upstairs in the kitchen, he read through the notebook by the lantern light again and found that Victor had an icehouse just outside the pantry's back entrance—likely a delivery door. Again, he drummed the page with a finger, as if tapping it might instill it into his memory. Walking through the pantry, he opened the door and stepped outside. Just to the left, a building, much like a barn danced in the lamplight.

When he got to the outside door, he found himself again trying keys, at least seven this time. He marked the icehouse key with a different bit of cloth and pulled the double doors open. A blast of cold air greeted him. He leaned in and held the lantern high. Large, uncut ice blocks were stacked against the back wall, three high, with the bottom ones partly buried in the ground. No doubt Victor had dealings with East India Company. The floor was dirt, though it did look raked and even. No windows, just a small vent cut into the roof. The space was large, and except for some ice-cutting and -moving tools, the ice blocks, as well as a large table, it was empty. If he moved the table, he could just back the cart in and leave it. The temperature had dropped to freezing, and snow had begun to fall in heaves and swirls. He wasn't worried about the body or Victor's head.

The captain walked the short distance back to the cart and drove it around to the icehouse and backed it in through the double doors. There, he unhitched the horse and tied it to some trees just a few yards from the icehouse. He went back, grabbed his bags and blankets, and locked the doors. He threw two large blankets over the horse's back before returning to the house. Along the way, he remembered something. Something important. Victor had money, money he could use to fund this venture that couldn't be traced back to him. He opened the notebook and thumbed through the pages, and then remembered he read about the money in a letter.

Inside, the captain made his way up the first set of narrow stairs to a hallway, where he found several empty rooms and two bedrooms.

He chose the larger room because it had a fireplace with wood stacked beside it. He lit a fire, stripped to his long johns, and sat in a chair near the hearth, a blanket wrapped over his shoulders, nibbling jerky as he waited for the water to boil. When the water was hot, the captain made himself strong cup of tea, which he sipped as he read through the letters. He found the one where Victor described to his sister that he'd amassed quite the fortune traveling and that he would be sending more by the week's end. The whole letter was cryptic and vague, but some details stood out—like fact the money wasn't in a bank or other financial institution. During one of their many conversations, Victor had stated off-hand that money was better kept within easy reach. Since Victor didn't carry more cash than he needed, this had to mean somewhere close by, which meant the money was here in the castle. His thoughts gave way to dreams.

Chapter 6: Chance Encounter

Cambridge, England: Cambridge Inn

The next day, the captain was up early. He spent the morning drinking tea and tidying the old castle, removing coverings, dusting and sweeping, and looking for ideal hiding places, of which there were many, and searching them. After several hours, he'd made his way to the lab. In the morning light, the room was cavernous, with mechanisms lining the walls. He noted lightning rods near the opening in the roof and several smaller versions attached to the table. He cleaned and searched. As he swept the floor, he noticed that under the table, near the platform's edge, he noticed a crank and handle, which he assumed to be a way to turn the table. He knelt to inspect these. When, with some effort, he turned the crank, the platform lifted. Once it was high enough, the captain saw the handle belonged to a hatch, which he tried to lift, but it was too heavy. He looked around and found a prybar and used that to lift the heavy hatch. Inside, the captain found several bags of cash. He pulled one out and opened it. He'd never seen so much money in one place before. There had to at least a thousand pounds in this bag, and there were four more just like it. He took five hundred and put the bag back.

As the captain ate lunch, he thought about the next step. He couldn't bring Victor back to life alone. The captain had figured out quite a bit of Victor's process from reading the notebooks, but he had limitations. Nautical things he understood well, but biological sciences held him hostage. Where to go? Who to ask? Would they think him mad? The risks of this venture had quite the opposite effect on him than he'd expected. He found himself eager, even excited, to get started. Cambridge was a few hours' ride, and there was a small standing of scientific minds in attendance, more so than Oxford, where most students went into the clergy. Aye, he'd travel this day to enlist the help he needed and had a few hours' journey to plan how that might happen or, if they thought him mad, how to escape. He'd find some eager, brilliant students and coerce them with stories of publication and invention; and if he had to, he'd bribe them. He readied a bag—a suit he'd taken from Victor's closet, some jerky and bread, a canteen of water, the cash—and his horse and set out by early afternoon, keeping a steady pace.

By early evening he'd arrived in Cambridge and found lodging at a local inn with a stable for his horse. The hostler took the horse, and the captain tipped him a thruppence.

"Thank you, governor!" the hostler said and led the horse away. The captain went into the inn.

A round, little woman with bright gray eyes and a big toothless smile greeted him. "Help you, sir?"

"Aye," the captain answered, "I'd like a room."

"Of course, of course, sir. Come right in."

The captain followed the woman and watched as her skirts swished, showing him glimpses of her ankles. She and her ankles disappeared behind a desk, where she pulled out a register.

"I'm Miss Harrow." She smiled. "How long will you be

staying?" she asked.

He nodded. "Nice to make your acquaintance, I'm sure. I should be just a night or two."

"All right, then. Just sign the register." She turned the book to face him, and he dipped the quill into the ink and signed. "Thank you," she said, turning the register so she could read it. "Captain. That'll be one thruppence for two nights."

The captain fished the money from his pocket and paid, then headed upstairs behind her, bag in hand.

"This is it. Enjoy your stay, and if you need anything, just let me know."

"Thank you," he said and entered the room, closing the door behind him. The room was clean. A bed and a dresser sat side-by-side. A small table with a lantern was situated on the other side of the bed. Near the window stood a wooden chair and table adorned with a doily and a pitcher and basin with a cloth folded nearby. He set the bag on the chair and looked out the window. He could see the university—or at least some of the castle-like buildings. He'd make his way there in the morning.

After he'd settled into the room and hung the suit over the chair, he dusted himself off, splashed some water in his face, and made his way to the inn's dining room to have a meal. The atmosphere teemed with activity, and there were more people than he'd expected. Besides a few lads who tipped a few too many pints, he noted the majority of patrons were single men, holding the latest news, eating a mutton stew, apparently the house specialty—its only specialty. The captain tried to decipher if these men were from Cambridge University, but he only noted one man with a book. A barmaid came to the table.

"What'll it be, sir? Mutton stew or eggs and beans? Ale or tea?" she offered.

The captain looked up. Her thin frame lost under her plain gray dress served to accentuate her dull blue eyes; there he saw no spark at all. When she smiled at him, it was forced, and he could see the faint lines around her mouth and eyes.

"Stew and tea, please," he said.

She nodded and left.

A stalky man in a gray suit stopped at his table, a newspaper under his arm. "University man?" he asked.

The captain, a bit startled by the intrusion, looked up. "No, no. But I am interested in the medical studies," he said.

"Oh, yes, yes," the man said, shaking the captain's hand. "Name's Doctor Jake Roberson. We have one of the finest medical facilities in all of England or Scotland. Mind if I join you?"

The captain couldn't believe his good fortune. He smiled. "Aye, by all means." He gestured toward the empty chair. "Good to know you, Doctor Roberson. People just call me Captain."

Dr. Roberson sat just as the barmaid brought the captain his meal. "Excuse me, miss. I'd like another cup of tea."

The barmaid nodded and was off again.

"So, what interest have you, obviously a seafaring man, in the medical field?" Dr. Roberson asked.

The captain sipped tea and swallowed the mouthful before he spoke, thinking he should have changed clothes. "That obvious, eh? And, aye, very true. I'm an explorer recently returned from the Arctic Circle and the North Sea. But that's my point. I've seen and learned much being at sea for so long. I have an interest in aiding my sailors when they fall ill and wish to learn anatomy and opiate medicines."

The barmaid arrived with the tea and set it before the doctor, who waved her away and picked up his cup.

"Yes, that would be helpful so far from land and good care. Opiates are all the rage in medicine presently. I regularly advise opium tincture or laudanum and take it myself when the occasion arises." He placed a hand on his jaw. "Opiates help many ailments." He set his cup down on the table.

"Fascinating. I'm heading to the university in the morning," the captain said, wiping his mouth and pushing the empty stew bowl aside. "Can you offer some direction?"

Dr. Roberson smiled, his white mustache wiggling over his upper lip like a shaggy caterpillar, seeming quite taken by his own authority on the subject. "I can do better than that, Captain. I'll give you the grand tour."

"That would be perfect. Is half seven all right, in front of the inn?"

"Yes, that's fine. I usually get to my lectures by nine, so that will give us a little time to talk."

"Very good, then," the captain said, reaching to shake the doctor's hand.

Dr. Roberson gave a firm shake. "See you then." He tossed a few shillings on the table and left the dining room.

The captain looked at the coins. His meal with tea added to the two teas the doctor had wouldn't cost that much. Even if the good doctor had eaten, it was still too much. He stood, feeling outdone and somewhat embarrassed. Fishing in his pocket, he added a thruppence.

The barmaid picked up the coins, and a genuine light passed across those dull eyes and she smiled. "Thank you, kind sir. Thank you!" she said and hurried away as if he might change his mind about paying so much. He didn't.

In his room, he lay on the bed and doused the lantern. He read through Victor's notes and letters in his mind. What luck he'd had meeting Dr. Roberson. Maybe there was such a thing as a predestined future after all. Or maybe the meeting was just pure luck. *Perhaps I won' be able to sleep*, he thought as he played with the next day's plans and how he might accomplish them, but then he did.

Chapter 7: George Kensington

Cambridge, England: Cambridge University Medical Facility

The next morning, the captain put on the suit and smoothed the jacket. In his front jacket pocket, he placed the wallet with two hundred pounds. In his trouser pocket, a hundred more and some change. He combed his hair back—not something he preferred to do—and locked the door on his way out.

Downstairs, the captain passed Miss Harrow. "Good morning, Miss Harrow."

She nodded, writing in a book. "Good morning; tea and potage in the dining hall this morning," she said, glancing at him.

"Thank you, but I'm in a bit of a hurry," he said, heading for the door. "I'll be out for some time. Feel free to make up the room."

"Always happy to oblige, Captain," she said.

Outside, the day was dark and heavy clouds hung low, threatening rain or possibly snow. Standing by a horse and buggy, Dr. Roberson smiled when he noticed the captain.

"I admire a punctual man," he said and gestured to the buggy, as the captain walked up. "Shall we?"

Though the captain thought the ride unnecessary with the campus such a short distance away, he climbed in. "Of course," he said.

The buggy ride took them through the center of the pastoral university campus, and the captain began to realize why the good doctor chose to ride. The medical facility, located at the rear of the campus, may have once housed something other than students and reminded him of a stone barn. The buggy pulled up in front of a staircase leading to large double doors.

"Here we are," said Dr. Roberson. "Follow me."

The captain followed the doctor in through the heavy doors just as light snow began to fall. The area, like a vast entry, had just one table and one room. To either side were staircases. One large oriel with a stone sill off the landing on the second floor above him, despite closed shutters, let in a draft. At the desk, an elderly woman with a white bun wearing a plain blue sensible dress and glasses sat writing, the edges of the paper held down with a rock so the occasional draft wouldn't send them to the stone floor. Several people, looking scholarly to the captain, gathered just inside the room.

Dr. Roberson said, "Looks delightfully barren, doesn't it?"

The question, the captain understood, was rhetorical. He smiled.

"That wonderful woman at the desk is our medical librarian, but she also helps students and professors with many other tasks. Her name is Miss Jackson." He gestured toward the people in the room. "Those are the medical facilities staff, but I won't bore you with introductions." He eyed the captain. "You did say you were most interested in anatomy and opiate medicines, correct?"

The captain nodded. "Aye, exactly so."

"Good, good. Then follow me because that's my area of expertise."

The captain followed the doctor, though not up any stairs as he'd anticipated. Instead, they crossed the room to a door, which he opened. He then lifted a lantern from an inside wall hook. He lit it and stepped into the room. A narrow staircase led down into darkness.

"The stairs can be a bit tricky even in daylight," he said and started down the steps.

At the bottom, the room opened into a cavernous basement. A large blackboard with chalk writing that filled it from top to bottom and had underlinings in different colors stood at the back of the room, where several tables with chairs sat. On the far side of the room, several lanterns hung around a single large table. The definitive shape of a human body lay under a cloth. A small table with a tray on top also had a towel over it, but the captain could tell instruments of some kind lay beneath.

"This is breathtaking," the captain said.

"It is, isn't it." Dr. Roberson agreed. "This is where the excitement is, where knowledge is honed and transferred; this is where I make science happen."

The captain noted something like arrogance in Dr. Roberson's voice. "Do you only teach anatomy?"

Dr. Roberson's eyes came back into focus. "No, not at all. I teach medicinal homeopathic plant medicine. As I'm sure you know, we use that to help with pain and healing." He walked over to the captain. "I teach everything scientific in this room." His eyes went dreamy again.

"Excellent," the captain said. "What about chemistry?"

"Indeed. I consider myself a chemist." He smiled. "I'm an all-around doctor, Captain, with expertise in many areas."

"Then I would like a chance to observe all of your lectures before I must take my leave, if that suits you."

"Indeed, it does!" His eyes refocused. "Come. Have a seat here at the back of the room so you can witness my students' reactions to my lecture; today's lecture includes anatomy, chemistry, and medicines. They are like rags soaking up the knowledge; it really is a sight to behold. Then you can join us in the laboratory to observe today's anatomy and chemistry lessons."

"Very good," the captain said and took a seat at the rear of the lecture area.

A short time later, Miss Jackson appeared with a small tray and set it before him.

"Dr. Roberson said you might like a spot of tea while you observe the goings-on," she said.

"Thank you kindly, Miss Jackson. I would indeed."

After she'd gone, he poured a cup of tea and waited, the anticipation growing like a winding spring in his gut. As he sipped his tea and watched Dr. Roberson wipe and scribble on the board, the students began to arrive, and he sized up each one as they settled into their chairs. They all seemed motivated by the time Dr. Roberson's lecture started.

Gesturing dramatically, his voice rising and falling, he pointed at the blackboard, pounded the desk, opened and closed books, and showed drawings and illustrations. His emotions moved the students, whose attention was focused on every word, every movement, their eyes wide with expectation and wonder... all except one—a young, dark-haired man with thick glasses, who worked at a feverish pace to scribble every word the doctor said on-to paper, sweat prickling his forehead and brow, some sliding from his hairline to stain his white collar. He stopped now and again to shake his wrist and begin anew. The captain thought the young man matched the doctor's energy and the intensity with which Victor must have scribbled his notes, and that, he knew, would be what he needed.

Later, he watched the young man while Dr. Roberson peeled back skin to discuss the contents of the human abdomen. If the young man got any closer, the captain thought he'd fall into the cavity. When Dr. Roberson pulled a length of intestines from the cadaver's abdomen like an enormous and hideous dead, gray worm, the memory of Victor's gut splitting and spilling to the ship's floor made the captain retch. As luck would have it, no one noticed.

After the anatomy lesson, the doctor dismissed most of the class and led him and the few remaining students to a cramped area behind a heavy curtain. Plants of all kinds in pots lined a stepped table; laboratory equipment, bubbling and dripping, was situated on a long table, reminding him of Victor's lab at the castle; and small bottles of pills and liquids filled shelving behind that table.

"This, Captain, is where I teach students the opium plant's medicinal properties and chemistry." Dr. Roberson opened a vile containing a deep red liquid. "This is the liquid form of laudanum."

The captain sniffed. "That's strong," he said.

The doctor nodded. "Indeed." He put the vial back on the table and gathered the group of students, including the dark-haired young man, in front of the plant table.

While Dr. Roberson and the students were distracted by demonstrations, the captain put several vials and bottles into his pockets. He slid a book off the shelf and opened it; it was authored by Dr. Roberson.

"Would you like to borrow it?" Dr. Roberson asked. "The book? I wrote it myself."

The captain gazed up from the contents. "Could I? Just for a night? I'll return it first thing tomorrow."

"Yes, yes, my good man. Did you want a closer inspection of the plants or medicines?"

The captain wandered past the plant table, stooping to look over some poppy plants on the bottom shelf. "Are these opium poppies?"

"Indeed," Dr. Roberson said. "But these are mere seedlings. We have a greenhouse for that purpose. Poppies can get two to three feet tall, and we couldn't accommodate them in this small space, now could we?" He laughed.

"I expect not." The captain pocketed two of the small seedlings before he stood and faced the doctor. "Thank you, doctor, for this fine adventure and the book. I shall return it first thing."

"My pleasure," Dr. Roberson said.

The captain shook the doctor's hand and took his leave—except he didn't leave. He stood outside near some trees and waited for the dark-haired young man to exit. While he waited, he thumbed through the doctor's opiate medicine text and thought he would pen much of this when he returned to the inn.

When he glanced up from the book, the young man he'd been waiting for finally exited the building, books shoved under his arm and papers fluttering in one hand. The young man hurried down the stairs and began toward wherever his next class might be. He needed to make a friend of this young man and fast.

"Excuse me? Young man?" the captain said.

"Me, sir?"

"Aye."

The young walked back to where the captain stood. "You were the bloke in lecture today, right?"

"Aye. And I would like to talk to you. Do you have a moment?"

The young man mulled this over. "What's this about, then?"

"It's about a proposition. I noticed you're quite the note taker, a detail-oriented young man. Would you like to make some cash, maybe have a hand in something new in medicine?

The young man's dark brown eyes lit with interest. "I might."

"You might, eh? What if I told you there'd be fame, fortune, and a reputation to be earned from it? What if I said you'd get paid an advance right now. Would you be interested then?"

The young man moved closer. "*That* does interest me."

"Good." The captain laid a hand on the young man's shoulder and dug in his pocket with the other. He pulled out five pounds and handed the money to the stunned young man. "Meet me this evening at eight for dinner at the Cambridge Inn dining room."

The young man's knees buckled and teetered, his mouth gaped, but he reached out an unsteady hand and took the money, then stared at it. "I certainly will."

"You can call me Captain, mate. What should I call you?"

"My name is George Kensington."

"Alright, Mister Kensington, tonight then."

"Call me George," he said, folding the money into his pocket.

"George, then."

George nodded and continued the trek he'd begun when the captain interrupted him, papers flapping as he hurried away. The captain watched for a few more moments, then turned to walk back to the inn.

Chapter 8: When a Plan Comes Together...

Cambridge Inn, England

That evening, the captain, dressed in usual pants, well-worn boots, and a flannel shirt, with his captain's hat on the back of his chair, sat at a far back table. The notebook lay on the table, his hand lying over it as if to guard it. He had enough money in his pocket to buy them both dinner and drinks, as well as to further bribe young George with the façade of a fund for the project that would pay for his absence at the university, the experience of which he could use as hours toward his education and, of course, with the supportive Dr. Roberson's blessing, which he would earn when he returned the book in the morning before departing.

George arrived promptly at eight—a good sign. He stood looking around the room for some time until the captain caught his attention, waving him over. George hurried to the table and sat.

"Good evening, Captain," he said.

The captain noted good posture and a serene disposition, though one hand busily flipped a coin between the knuckles, back and forth. "Good that you made it, George. I've ordered food with tea. Perhaps we'll sip some ale later?"

"Thank you, Captain. That would be nice."

The barmaid arrived with two bowls of stew, rough bread, and two hot teas.

"Thank you, miss," the captain said, then turned his attention to George, who was already eating like he hadn't had a bite in days. The captain decided to wait until they'd finished their meal before he broke the ice.

With the dishes cleared and two pints of ale between them, the captain tapped on the notebook. "I'm sure you're anxious to learn what project awaits you," he said and opened the notebook.

George nodded and pulled from his jacket a quill and ink, which he set up in an orderly fashion. He dipped the quill in the ink and readied to write. "I am, sir, very anxious and excited."

The captain smiled. "You needn't take notes at this meeting, George. I have everything we need in this notebook." He tapped the notebook with his index finger.

"Oh, right, sir. Sorry, sir." He put the supplies away and focused on the captain.

"This book," the captain began, "belonged to a man of science and exploration named Victor Frankenstein. Have you heard of him?"

George took several gulps of his ale and leaned closer to the captain. "I have, sir. The whole fiasco is quite up in the air, you know. The public, the officials, and the university hotly debate what the truth is, but we agree that Frankenstein had troubles with a large, deformed man who murdered members of his family, among many others…" George put the ale to his lips, held it there, then drank the mug dry. "I understand that he traveled after enduring a prolonged official inquiry from which he was found innocent of any involvement with the monster. I know his castle was searched more than once in the early part of last year, and the castle is believed to be abandoned. I know he has not returned. No one really knows what happened or where he or the monster are now."

"That about sums most of it up." The captain waved the barmaid over and ordered more ale for George, who seemed grateful enough when it arrived. "What would you say if I could tell you the rest of the story, the truth? What if I told you Victor was onto something larger than life itself?"

George was toying with the coin again and gazing into the ale mug. "You said 'was' onto something. Past tense." He drained the cup.

"Aye. That's because I was there, in the Arctic, when Victor Frankenstein died."

The barmaid showed up with two more cups of ale, and George down half before he spoke again. "How is that possible, Captain?" he asked and looked up.

"Because I found Victor sledding across the ice in pursuit of the monster. *His* monster, George."

George polished the mug of ale and lost control of the coin he'd been flipping; it bounced to the floor, spun, and dropped. He leaned to fetch it and almost fell from the chair. He straightened himself and asked, "What does this have to do with your proposition, Captain?"

The captain slid his mug of ale over to George. "Everything." He pushed the notebook across the table. "Read, and then we'll talk some more."

George opened the notebook and began to read.

The captain watched how George's facial expressions changed

from moment to moment, how he toyed with the coin, how he gulped the ale, how the sweat trickled from his hairline, and how his foot bounced as if a fire had been built beneath him. He waited, sipping tea, for that moment when the hammer would drop.

Three cups of tea later, George looked up and closed the notebook, but he didn't take his hand from the cover. He leaned forward and whispered, "This is… The monster, then? Frankenstein's creation?"

"Aye."

"And the notes penned into the last pages, these are yours?"

"Aye."

He pushed the notebook across the table. "I want to know more."

"And you will." He pulled fifty pounds from his wallet and slipped the notes into the notebook and pushed it back to George. "This will be just the beginning of the funding for the project, for your services. If you take it and come with me to Victor's castle, your name will be on the lips of men for all of history. You will be a father of scientific discovery." The captain saw the light of eagerness shine in George's eyes, and he knew he had the young man hook, line, and sinker.

"I want to go; it's the opportunity of a lifetime," George said and slipped the pages from the notebook, then quickly folded them and put them into his front pocket.

"Aye, it is. Meet me in front of the medical building tomorrow at noon. Bring all that you need for at least two weeks; we won't have time to dawdle. We should make the castle by dusk." He held out his hand.

George stood, wobbled, and shook the captain's hand. "Tomorrow then," he said and left, tripping over the threshold as he walked out onto the street.

The captain picked up the notebook, put on his hat, and left two shillings on the table.

In the lobby, Miss Harrow busied herself at the desk when he walked past, heading upstairs.

"Good night, sir," she said.

The captain stopped and looked back. "Good night, Miss Harrow." He started to climb and stopped again. "Can you bring tea in about an hour? Oh, and Miss Harrow, I'll be leaving in the morning. Thank you for your hospitality."

"Of course, sir."

Back in the room, the captain lit the lamp and started a fire and sat in the chair by the window with a blanket over his shoulders, reading Dr. Roberson's book. Victor's notebook lay open on the table, and the captain would jot notes as he read and drew tiny illustrations of plants. The carefully wrapped opium poppy seedlings were on the table, and the medicine vials had been stored in his bag.

The knock on the door startled him, and he checked the Verge Fusee pocket watch. That would Miss Harrow with his tea. "It's open. Come in."

Miss Harrow entered carrying a tray with a tea service and set it on the table. "Anything else, sir?" she asked.

"No, thank you. This is quite nice."

"I put a couple of biscuits on the side. You can just leave the tray, sir. I'll have it collected in the morning after you leave. Good night, sir."

"Goodnight, Miss Harrow."

The captain made the tea and continued his work with Dr. Roberson's book until the early hours of the morning. When he'd completed his study of the book, he locked the bedroom door, crawled under the covers, doused the lamp, and closed his eyes.

Chapter 9: Best Laid Plans...

Cambridge, England: Cambridge University Medical Facility

The captain woke early, though he'd had very little sleep. As he packed, all he could think about was getting back to Victor's lab, which surprised him because most of the time, all he could think about was getting back to the sea, back to exploring. The sea had always been his mistress. He read the pocket watch before he put it into his jacket's breast pocket. He still had some time to eat breakfast and check out before heading to the university to talk to Dr. Roberson. If he caught him before nine this morning, he'd have enough time to convince him that he needed George and that he should allow credit. He felt there was a good chance Dr. Roberson could be bribed with a donation to the medical facility.

The captain grabbed his bag and went downstairs to check out. Miss Harrow, whom he thought at this point never left the desk, stood with her back to him, fussing with something behind the desk. *Maybe the mail,* he thought.

"Any message for me?" the captain asked.

She started and spun around. "Oh, Captain! You scared me! I didn't hear you coming." She composed herself. "No mail, sir. Checking out?"

"Aye, I'm afraid so. I've got to get back to London."

"Ah, yes. Your business is done then, is it?" she asked, opening the cash box.

"Aye, it is." He paid his bill, leaving her a generous tip.

"Thank you, Captain. It's been a pleasure to serve you, and I hope you come back to see us again soon." She smiled. "Breakfast before your travels? Biscuits and potage? Tea, perhaps?"

"Aye, I think I will. It's a long ride."

After he ate, he visited the stable and retrieved his horse; he packed up and headed over to the university, where he tied the horse to a tree in front of the medical facility before going inside.

Dr. Roberson was right where the captain expected him to be, in the lecture hall writing on the blackboard.

"Excuse me, Doctor Roberson?"

Dr. Roberson turned, his cheeks blooming red, but when he saw it was the captain, his mood brightened. "Captain! You've come back; that's marvelous." He rushed over and put an arm around the captain's shoulder. "Did you like the book?"

The captain, somewhat uncomfortable, shook himself loose and turned to face the doctor. "Aye, it was fascinating and informative. Well written indeed."

"Well, thank you. I invested a lot of time in that book, and it's being used often at various universities as a teaching tool. Quite remarkable, really."

"That's quite amazing," the captain said, moving toward the back of the room. "Can we talk somewhat more privately? Perhaps in the chemistry room? That way, I can return the book to its place."

"That's a good idea. Saves me the trouble."

The two men retreated behind the curtain, and the captain returned the book to the shelf. "Listen, I have a science experiment I'm working on in London. It's rather secretive and is a new exploration."

"Oh, I do love innovations. What are you studying?"

"Well, doctor, that's the secret. I do, however, have a proposal for you."

"I'm intrigued," he said and leaned against a table.

"Glad to hear that because I need the services of one of your students for a few weeks—"

Dr. Roberson stood straight. "What? No, that's just not—"

The captain put a hand up. "Please, just hear me out before you make a final judgment."

"I suppose… What kind of donation are we talking about?"

Right to the money, the captain thought. "About three hundred pounds."

"That's quite a donation, Captain, but my students need to be here to learn." Dr. Roberson looked at his pocket watch. "Can we hurry this along. I must finish my lecture notes."

The captain moved closer to the doctor. "I want to use George Kensington. Just two weeks. I think three hundred quid should cover his absence, and he will learn a lot he can bring back to the classroom, to you, doctor."

"Yes, it probably would, but I'm the professor, the expert in these areas, so I think you should just invite me. I can put off classes for two weeks for that kind of money."

"I don't need an expert for this project, doctor. I know exactly what I'm doing. I just need a knowledgeable helping hand, and this is something young George could learn from, become a better student of science and medicine. I would think just assisting would be beneath your station as headmaster."

"That may be the case, Captain, but it is also beneath my students. Perhaps you can garner a helper from the London streets. My students are learning medicine, and they will become doctors. Doctors are not helpers, sir; they're professionals."

The doctor moved to exit, and the captain stepped in front of him.

"George is not yet a doctor, and from what I've learned, he is in his second year, with many more to come. This project would be perfect for him. I can't use just any help. I need someone who can understand and perform what I'm asking."

"Please stand aside, Captain. I have a class. The answer is no, and that's my final word on the subject."

"I'm sorry to hear that, Doctor, because George is coming with me; he's already been paid. Just take the donation. He'll be back before you know it."

Fever rose in the doctor's cheeks, and his lips peeled back from his teeth, his mustache rising to meet his nose. "He will do no such thing! If he so much as steps one foot off this campus, I'll have him dismissed immediately! Now stand aside!"

Dr. Roberson put a hand on the captain's arm and tried to shove him away from the curtain. The captain reacted by pushing him back into the table, where the stunned doctor straightened and brushed off his jacket.

"If you don't step aside, sir, I'll have you removed."

"I'd like to see that, mate."

The doctor tried to rush past the captain, shoving him. "Miss Jackson! Miss Jackson! Go for help!"

The captain clamped a hand over the doctor's mouth and pulled him back. They struggled, and the captain pushed him to the floor, and the captain's hand slipped.

"Help! Murder!"

The captain punched the doctor and loomed over him. He punched the doctor again and again, the blood spraying and dotting his face and clothes and smearing across the doctor's face.

"Please…stop!" the doctor moaned, his voice garbled and his mouth filled with blood.

"It's too late for that, I'm afraid," the captain said, reaching for a pair of nearby pruning shears. They rose above his head and came down with a sickening *thud*. The doctor gasped, the fear and surprise in his eyes gave the captain hesitation, but he knew it was too late to turn back now. The captain pulled the shears out and brought them down again and again, spraying blood across his shirt, the wall, and the ceiling. The doctor struggled and gasped but couldn't scream. When the captain stopped, the doctor looked at him; he gurgled, blood bubbling from his mouth and nose, then the light left his eyes. The captain, still on his knees, rolled away, tossing the shears aside, and lay staring at the blood-splattered ceiling, his breathing ragged. His vision ticked from the ceiling to the nearby tables and beyond. Blood everywhere. This was not something he'd have time to clean up. He'd have to leave the body and get out as quickly as possible. It wouldn't be long before the doctor's body would be discovered.

The captain stood. He grabbed a rag and turned to a water basin nearby. He wet the cloth and began scrubbing his face and hands until they were clear of gore. He wiped the blood off his boots and made some attempt to wipe it off his clothes, but this only smeared the blood. Frustrated, he gave it up and tossed the rag into the garbage bin, then dumped the dirty water into the planters. As fast as he could manage, he scooped up more seedlings, medicines, books, and notes, and shoved them into a nearby bag. He pushed the doctor's body under the table so it couldn't be seen from beyond the curtain, then hurried into the lecture area. No students had arrived, and he felt some relief. An overcoat laying over a chair back caught his eye. He grabbed it and put in on as he hurried up the steps and made his way to the exit.

"Good day, sir," Miss Jackson said. "Safe travels."

The captain's stomach knotted. Without stopping, he said, "Thank you, Miss Jackson, and good day." Without missing a step, he hurried out the doors to his waiting horse, which he mounted and walked it away from the entrance. The sounds of hooves against stone turned his attention from the building, and he saw a single horse-drawn buggy approaching. He realized this was George. He moved to intercept.

"Whoa!" the captain said, pulling the reins. "Ready?"

George stopped the buggy. "I am. Did you speak to Doctor Roberson yet?"

The captain noted a large trunk and several bags in the back of the buggy and decided these must include everything George had from the university dorms. "Aye. We're good to go."

"Good, then," George said and turned the buggy around.

"Just follow me," the captain said and set the pace at a steady trot.

Chapter 10: It's Too Good to be True

London, England: Victor Frankenstein's Castle

That evening, after George and the captain arrived and settled into Victor's castle, the two men sat in the living area near the fire, sipping hot tea and eating biscuits.

"This place," George began and sipped from his teacup. "My family owns a mansion, but this place… It's magical."

"It does have that effect. I felt much the same way when I arrived," the captain said, adjusting the blanket around his shoulders. "We should talk about the notebook. What did you think?"

George mulled this over, sipping tea. "Well, at first I thought it fiction, good fiction actually, but it dawned on me that it definitely wasn't that. I carefully studied the science and the medicine in the writing—and came to the sudden realization that this was an entirely new way of looking at life and death." He sipped his tea and bit into a biscuit. "I must admit the whole reanimation process has me fascinated. It's not like the theories haven't been proven, but Frankenstein did create a creature he couldn't control." He popped the remainder of the biscuit in his mouth. "What makes you think this time will be different?"

"When I first read through what Victor left behind, I too was skeptical, but when I studied the notebooks and letters—and you'll get to read the others in the morning over breakfast—I came to understand Victor's mistake. He'd taken the brain of an average man and placed it into a stitched-together body." He glanced at George, who'd stopped in mid-chew. "We've got Victor's brain." George's eyes widened, and his mouth opened and closed. The captain sipped his tea and let that revelation sink in. "It means, Georgie, mate, we have the brain of a scientific genius this time around."

George sipped the tea and swallowed with an audible gulp. "Ho-how do we have Victor's brain exactly?"

"He died in the artic at temperatures below zero. He froze, his brain preserved. It's in the icehouse around back. With temperatures dropping and winter almost upon us, the bodies are still well-preserved."

"That's…incredible!" George said, pouring more tea into his cup. "I've read some literature on this type of thing, preservation of the brain." He stopped short before pouring in the milk, the jug hovering over the cup. "But what about the body. The notes provide that the creature's body was made up of several newly dead men—"

"Not a problem, young man. We also have the creatures preserved body. All we need do is put Victor's brain in his own creation's body and bring him back."

George's cup rattled against the saucer, and the milk splashed into the cup. "So, what you're saying is that we're actually ready to move forward with the reanimation process." He steadied the cup and set the milk jug down on the tray.

"Aye, we are, almost. I need you to study the notebooks Victor wrote in as he reanimated the creature. The science is beyond my understanding."

"Ah, I see. You need my medical expertise, except I'm still a student, Captain. Wouldn't it have been easier to ask Doctor Roberson to conduct the experiment?"

"Maybe easier, but he wasn't right for the job. Besides, you have what it takes. I could tell from the moment I laid eyes on you, George. Doctor Roberson was for the living; you were made to resurrect the dead."

George set his cup down on the table. "Well, I'm grateful you feel that way, and I will endeavor to do my best."

"I know you will, George." The captain stood. "Now, get some rest. We've a big day tomorrow."

George yawned and stood. "Good night, Captain."

"Good night, George."

Early the next morning at breakfast, George ate, absorbed in the notebooks. The captain decided he liked the intensity at which George read and jotted notes. Aye, this was the man for the job without any doubt.

"How's it going, mate?" the captain asked.

"Brilliantly," George said.

"So, you're able to decipher the science and the method?"

"Absolutely brilliant."

"Right, then. I'll go work on the lab, and you can join me there when you're ready. Looks like we might be on for tonight, if you can help make that happen. Did you see the sky today?"

George looked up. "I did. Dark and dreary, I'm afraid. Looks like a storm's headed our way."

"Exactly."

Realization washed across George's face. "Right, yes! We'll need some lightning for this task. I'll join you shortly," he said and resumed reading.

The captain refilled his tea and made his way to the lab to set up the experiment. He readied the table with fresh cloth and boiled the instruments for the operation. As he did so, a light rain began to fall, so he covered the table and instruments with a tarp. He'd gotten the mechanical chain that closed the hatch over the opening to work before he'd left. Now, he stood at the wheel and turned it with some effort until the hatch was sufficiently closed. It leaked, but it would hold until they needed it opened.

He'd left the bags with the seedlings and opium-based medicines on the floor. He now unpacked those. He placed the seedlings near the fireplace to keep them warm and alive; the medicines he placed on a shelf. As for his part, he was ready. They just needed to get the creature's body and Victor's head inside to thaw by nightfall.

George bounded down the stairs, the notebooks under one arm and a teacup in the other hand. He laid the lot on the table. "Shall we go get our subjects then?"

"If we want them thawed enough in time, aye, we should," the captain agreed.

The two men made their way out to the icehouse, where they unpacked the creature down to the bottom crate in which the body lay. The captain set the small wooden box with Victor's head inside on top of the body.

"We'll just pull this in like a sled. I'll pull, and you push. Just keep it steady for me, mate," the captain said.

"Right."

George and the captain pulled the makeshift sled out of the icehouse and into the castle, but getting it down the steep, winding stairs to the laboratory proved harrowing. As they inched their way down, George kept pushing the crate with the head back into place.

"Stop for a minute, would you. I have an idea," George said. "Hand me the rope, and I'll hand you Victor's head, I mean, the crate. You run it downstairs, and I'll hold this pallet steady. Then we'll be able to move quite a bit easier."

"Good call." The captain reached back and the two exchanged holdings, a head for a rope. The captain set the crate on one of the tables and returned to help George get the creature's body down the remaining stairs.

Drenched in sweat, the men got the pallet placed close to the roaring fireplace and cut away the bindings and cloth. The captain stared at the creature; it looked the same as it had the day he'd found it; it astounded him that it was so well preserved. Next, the captain opened the crate. The water around the head had frozen solid, with the bags that once held the ice stuck firmly to it.

"Hand me that nail pull." He pointed. "Over there on the bottom of that rack."

George brought the captain the tool and watched in mesmerized horror and fascination as he pulled the crate away from the ice block with Victor's head frozen inside.

"It's pretty well preserved, wouldn't you say, mate?" the captain asked.

"I do see some blackening, frostbite, and decomposition on the chin, ears, and nose. A few spots on the cheek, but, yes, I think all of that is superficial. The brain should be well preserved," George said, leaning in for a closer look. "We'll need to watch over them. We don't want to cook anything."

The captain began laughing; he just couldn't help picturing Victor's head with an apple in the mouth and turning on a spit. "Right…"

George turned, and before he could protest the seriousness of what he'd said, he, too, broke into the laughter of a madman. "This is not professional," he said between bursts of laughter. "They say… it's natural to laugh when stressed." He glanced at the captain, who glanced back.

Then they laughed even harder. "Isn't that hysteria or something?" the captain asked.

"So some believe," George said.

After some time, the laughter subsided, and the two men settled in to watch the ice melt, something both new would take all day and into the evening. Occasionally, one or the other would head upstairs to bring food and drink down for them both. They stoked the fire and moved their subjects around as if they were indeed roasting them.

George stood over Victor's head. "He's done, I believe, Captain."

The captain held back a laugh and walked over to inspect the head. "Aye, I believe so. Let's move it to the table. It needs to stay cool while we wait on the body."

George moved to inspect the creature's body. "It's thawing evenly. We'll need to move it a bit closer and stoke up the fire, maybe turn him every fifteen minutes. He'll thaw faster that way."

For a moment, George's face seemed to crinkle, his eyes glazed, and then he relaxed. The captain realized their conversations since bringing the subjects from the icehouse had proven macabre at best and heinous at worst. It appeared their laughter was indeed stress-related. He supposed laughter was better than taking in the reality of what they were about to do, which was madness at worst and ground-breaking at best, and yet he knew neither of them could wait to do it.

"We should be sure there aren't any mirrored objects in the room," George said. "According to Victor's notes, it'd be too shocking at first. We'll need to ease Victor into seeing himself."

"Aye. He spoke at great lengths about the creature's reactions to its looks. Best I can tell, the creature never accepted its body. It just wanted a woman—Victor almost granted it that wish but changed his mind—someone to love and that it could love. Sad, really. It's what Victor believed caused it to murder his brother and then his fiancée. Victor just wanted to end the creature. And now…to become what he first loved then loathed… Well… It could be disturbing for him," the captain said, staring into the steaming cup.

"I can see that. But these notes can help us. We can help Victor to acclimatize to his new body. Perhaps there is some peace in knowing the creature is gone and he'll have the control that he didn't have before."

"Perhaps."

The fire had burned through several trees by the time they hefted the creature's body onto the table that evening. The storm had intensified over the last few hours. The captain heard thunder and saw lightning through cracks in the hatch, which was leaking like a sieve.

No point in mopping it up, though. He'd see to that chore after the storm cleared. George had taken the notebooks and had them laid out on a table. He mixed chemicals and checked notes. The captain could smell death and the promise of life in every breath.

When George finally spoke, it was with a confidence he'd not heard before.

"I'm ready. Let's begin," he said.

The captain watched with morbid curiosity as George made the scalp incision and, using a scalpel, peeled back the skin from the skull. With a steady hand, he began to saw the skull until it cracked like an egg; then, he cut the membrane, peeling it back like the petals of a closed flower, exposing the pale brain. What came next held the captain's gaze and commanded all of his attention. George poured three different chemical compounds from the vials he'd mixed into the brain cavity and over the brain, after which, he lifted the brain from its perch and put it in a dish, where he poured more of the chemical compounds over it. A snapping and popping noise followed, and the brain began to pulse and the liquid to bubble.

"Should it be bubbling that way?" the captain asked.

George grinned. "Exactly so. Now, we let it soak for a couple of hours so it can grow and awaken the cells." He looked at the notebook laid open on the counter. "Those cells are one of two keys," he said and took Victor's head to the fireplace, where he stoked the fire and dropped the head in. "That should be mostly ash by tomorrow." George wiped his hands on his pants and returned to the table.

The captain felt he should have been repulsed by this act, by the nonchalant manner in which George dropped part of a human being into a blazing fire. Still, George's enthusiasm for the experiment proved contagious, and all the captain could feel was the euphoria of excitement. "What two keys?"

"This is the mixture, the first key, Victor used on the organs and brain of the creature; he noted they promoted cell growth and connectivity, and when he stimulated a cell branch in the brain, some part of the body moved or an organ pulsed." He came around the table and showed the captain the notebook. "He said the brain stem connected to the spinal column." He tapped the page. "I read a paper about a new brain science, but it's widely unaccepted by the medical community. I assume, like all things academic, in time, we'll accept that the brain is the center of human life and definitely more important than the heart." He grinned wider. "I think, Captain, this is the experiment that could open this science and make it acceptable."

While he hadn't expected a speech, the captain was glad for it; it explained those puzzle pieces he'd been unable to work out reading the letters and notebooks. *George was very focused*, the captain thought. *Reminds me of Victor and the vitality of youth.*

"Those bubbles are the same spark that Frankenstein witnessed the night he brought his creature to life. They tell us the chemicals are working," George continued.

"So, what's the second key, then?"

George looked up and gestured toward the trap door in the roof. "Lightning." He gazed around the room and made a wide fanning gesture. "See these lightning rods? These are going to help us unlock life."

The captain gazed up, scratching his beard, and nodded. They were really going to do this, bring Victor back to life. He glanced at George. "Tea?"

George clapped him on the shoulder. "Excellent idea!"

The two men stood in the lab by the table, sipping tea and watching the brain bubble and listening to the storm rage.

"Victor was quite gifted in the sciences, but what's happening here is beyond my understanding," George said and leaned close to the bowl. "Do you see those little hair-like growths covering the brain?"

The captain set his cup on the table and leaned in. "What *are* those?"

"Those," George said, glancing at the captain, "are what we've been waiting for." He stood, drained his teacup, and set it aside. "Let's begin, shall we?"

Once again, the captain found himself unable to tear his gaze from the creature as George reopened the monster's skull, removed the brain, and placed Victor's pulsing brain into the cavity. George poured more of the liquid into the cavity and closed it up. The whole procedure took less than an hour. The captain moved the lightning rods closer to the four corners of the table. He and George tied metal bars between each rod and the table in a way that they touched some part of the creature's body. The two men looked at each other.

"That's it then," the captain said.

"We're ready," George said, gazing up. "Open the roof hatch."

The captain looked up at the dripping hatch, listened to the raging storm, and felt he should be welling with excitement of the sort that Victor described, that his veins should be running with anticipation. His heart pounded, threatening to burst through his chest. His temples throbbed in a way that made his eyes want to come out of their sockets. He looked from the door to the crank to the creature. "We'll get soaked."

"Yes, but isn't that part of the intrigue, the excitement?" George placed a hand on the captain's arm. "Listen, if you're worried about the creature, don't. He's strapped to the table. If you're worried about any backlash, don't. I take full responsibility for this experiment, whatever happens. You were right when you asked me to join you; this is the opportunity of a lifetime. We're about to make history for the second time, and people will take notice. Come for the ride. Let me take the risks."

"That's good of you, mate, but I'm in this for the long haul," the captain said, "This is my venture even more than yours; Victor was my friend. Let's just hope it is still Victor when the creature revives." He took a deep breath, crouched, and began to turn the crank.

It was slow-going, and the hatch doors opened inches at a time. The rain poured in and beat down on the tables and floor. The captain stood on the platform's edge near another crank that would elevate them to the roof, and George stood on the other side. He nodded at George, who nodded in return. The captain turned the crank, and the platform rose until it was level with the roof.

The rain whipped around them, and the wind howled. Thunder

boomed, followed within seconds by the crackles and streaks of blue-white lightning tearing across the night sky.

"Attach that long bar to the lightning rod!" the captain shouted.

George nodded and struggled with the bar.

"Hurry! We don't want to get struck!"

"I am! It's just stuck. Help me!"

The captain hurried around the table and helped George secure the long rod fixed to the table. He then made sure all the bars were touching each other and the creature. They stepped back, and the captain took hold of the level that raised the main lightning conductor rode. He pulled, and the lightning rod rose. The two men stepped away, backs against one of the raised walls.

The captain leaned close to George's ear. "Now, we wait!"

Lightning tore across the sky like webbing and bolts came to ground with resounding cracks. When the bolt struck the lightning conductor above them, George and the captain ducked the sparks that showered around them. The creature's neck and back arched as if lifted by invisible hands, its fists clenched, and its feet banged the table as though it was a child having a temper tantrum. It seemed to go on for a long while but lasted only seconds, seconds that ticked by as if in slow motion.

The captain pulled the lever and lowered the lightning rod, then he disconnected the bars, all while glancing at the night sky. He cranked as fast as he dared to lower the table. Once on the floor, he closed the hatch. The two men stood, breathing heavily, as rainwater dripped to the floor.

George pulled a mirror from his kit and held it in front of the creature's mouth and nose, while the captain watched to see if its chest rose and fell.

"I don't think it worked," George said. "The glass isn't fogging."

"I don't think it's breathing," the captain said, placing a hand on the creature's chest. At that moment, the captain realized this was no longer just a creature; if it woke, it would be Victor reborn. "The least we can do, in case he does recover, is dress him in some dry clothes."

The captain knew exactly where to find clothes that would fit the creature—a closet in Victor's room filled with oversized clothing that he—or someone—had stitched together.

"That's a good idea; it will at least make us feel better about all this. Maybe it takes a bit of time for the chemical reaction," George offered.

"Perhaps."

When the captain returned, the two men dried off the creature and the table, then with some difficulty, they dressed him.

George said, "What say we get dried and changed, too, and maybe grab some tea to warm up."

The captain watched the creature's chest. "I suppose if we don't, we'll catch our deaths."

PART II: Frankenstein Reborn

Chapter 1: An Unexpected Result

London, England: Victor Frankenstein's Laboratory

Victor's eyes fluttered open; a wooden hatch, water dripping like a leaky pipe and trickling in spastic streams swam into focus. A fire nearby crackled and snapped; he felt its radiating warmth and smelled the burning wood. Familiar, all of it…yet none of it. Disconnected thoughts whizzed through his mind, but they were vague, watery, as though he'd slept using opium. He tried to turn his head but realized a strap held his head in place. He tried to raise a hand but found that, too, was strapped, as were his legs. His mouth worked, and he tried to speak, to yell, but what he heard terrified him more than the straps.

A cup shattered somewhere behind him. Voices. When a face came into view, it was a familiar one. His mouth worked; he wanted to say, "Captain." Instead, that godawful guttural sound filled his ears.

"He's alive!" the captain said, placing a hand on the creature's hand. "Victor's alive!"

Another face came into view.

"He most assuredly is." George looked at the captain, his eyes widening. "We did it!" His laughter echoed through the lab, and he clapped the captain on the back. "We've made history!" George hurried to the counter, to the notebook, and began dipping and scribbling.

"You mean, we've made history again, mate." The captain looked into Victor's eyes; they were the same as they'd been in life but confused. "Victor? Can you hear me, mate? It's me, the captain. Remember?"

Again, Victor tried to speak, and again, all he heard was the guttural, nonsensical noise coming from his mouth. He nodded.

"George!"

George grabbed the notebook and the inked quill and joined the captain. "What is it?"

"Watch." The captain leaned closer to Victor. "Do you know where you are?"

Victor's mind, threading itself together, knew the answer: his laboratory. He nodded.

"See that, George? He understands."

"Yes, fascinating." He scribbled and leaned forward. "Victor, my name is George Kensington. I'm a friend of the captain." He glanced at the notebook. "Your voice should come back with time and a little practice."

Victor understood them, but his fragmented mind struggled to put together the scattered pieces of the recent past. He groaned again and fought against the straps.

"Easy, mate," the captain said. "It's going to take a bit of time for you to remember what happened and to regain the voice to speak it." He glanced at George, who was speed-reading through pages of a notebook. "Anything about this, George?"

George stood beside the captain. "In his notes, Vic—" He glanced at Victor. "He said that within hours things about the creature's life returned to him, and by the next day, he was speaking."

"I see," the captain said. He looked at Victor. "Try to relax and concentrate. Can you tell me your name?"

Victor stared at the hatch in the roof. Why was this idea of a creature so familiar? "Vi-c-tr," he said.

"Good. Very good," George said. "Try again."

Victor still didn't want to look at his old friend, so he continued to stare at the hatch. "Victor," he said again, clearer this time, but there was still a groaning quality to the speech.

"Good. Tell me where you are, Victor," George said.

Victor eased his gaze toward the two men—so much expectation in their eyes. Something terrible must have happened, an accident of some kind. His mind was grasping the now but still struggling with the then. "My…home. Castle… Laboratory."

"Excellent!" George glanced at the captain. "How about some food and a cup of tea to take the chill off, Victor?"

"Yes, food…tea," Victor said, trying to ignore how child-like he sounded…but this, too, seemed familiar.

"Right. I'll be back shortly."

Being restrained bothered Victor, though he didn't quite grasp why the straps or looking up at the hatch were familiar and somewhat exciting…and frightening. The answers, though, were close, like fishing for just the right words. He closed his eyes and ran through his flying and swirling thoughts, grabbing at pieces, pulling them together, trying to find an order of events. Visions of a boy laughing one moment and dead on the ground the next; a woman smiling while holding him one moment and in a bed, dead, the next; newspaper headlines; endless ice; this laboratory; a ship; the captain; notebooks, letters, and something else… A creature. But how did these pieces fit? He groaned. Whatever the order, his life didn't… What? End well? Did it end? His heart raced almost as fast as his mind. He couldn't breathe! Suffocating! He needed to get up! Had to get up! Twisting his hands and drumming his legs, he fought the straps, could hear them straining, pulling at the bolts that held them in place.

"Up! Up! Up!" he screamed.

A gentle hand found his shoulder. "Easy, mate," the captain said. "Lay still and I'll remove the straps, but you have to promise to stay calm, okay?"

Victor stilled, but his breaths came in gasps. "I will...be...calm."

The captain began undoing the straps, and George arrived with a tray of food and tea that he sat on a nearby table. He glanced at George with his hands poised on the last strap over Victor's forehead. George nodded, and the captain released the last strap.

Victor looked around and then at the captain and tried to sit without success. His body felt heavy and unfamiliar. He tried again but couldn't get quite upright. On the third try, the captain helped him sit at the edge of the table. For a moment, Victor held the captain's uncertain gaze, and then he looked down at his body, his hands, his feet... "What...*is this*?" he screeched and tried to stand on feet that weren't his own. His knees buckled, and he fell to all fours. "What's... happened to me?"

George and the captain crouched on either side of him and helped him to a stand.

"We'll explain that later. Right now, you should sit, mate. You've been down for quite a while. It might take a bit for your legs to be strong enough," the captain said.

Victor looked the captain in the eyes. Fear filled them. "Not here."

George brought over a straight-backed chair, and he and the captain helped Victor to sit. The chair groaned under his weight but held. "How about that tea?"

Victor looked at his hands and then at George. "Tea."

George went to hand Victor the cup, and the captain stepped in. "Let me," he said and took the cup. He crouched beside Victor.

"You might not be able to hold a cup as yet." He held the cup toward Victor.

Victor grasped the captain's hands in his own and pulled the cup to his mouth and sipped. "Good," he said and pulled the cup to his mouth again. This time he managed to finish the cup. "Thank you, Captain."

"You're quite welcome, mate." The captain handed George the cup. "You want to try a biscuit?"

"Yes," Victor said.

The captain put a slice of meat on a piece of bread and handed it to Victor.

Again, Victor closed his hands over the captain's and pushed the bread to his mouth.

"Better?" asked George.

"Better," said Victor. "Now, tell me what's happened."

The captain glanced at George, who shrugged. "One thing at a time, mate. You already sound better, so that's some progress, but maybe we should just get you moving and then get some sleep. It's been a long day. We can talk more in the morning," the captain said.

Victor sighed into his lap, a heavy wheezing noise. He gazed up at the captain. "Over breakfast?"

"Yes, mate. Over breakfast. Anything you want," the captain said. "We'll explain all we know, and we can go from there. Deal?"

Victor stared at his hands, some of the fragmented memories falling into place. A tear slid down his cheek. "Deal." He tried on a smile that came off a little sideways. "I want beans and a fried egg with toast."

The captain smiled. "Perfect choice, mate. And done."

George and the captain walked Victor around the room for another hour, stopping now and again to allow Victor to partake in tea, which he really enjoyed. Then they guided him up the stairs.

"Goodnight, gents," George said and walked down the hall to his room.

"Come on, Victor. This is your room," the captain said, guiding Victor into his bedroom. He helped Victor into bed. "I'll be just up the hall if you need anything," the captain said, gathering his things.

"Stay, Captain… At least for a while?"

The captain sat on the edge of the bed. "Sure, mate. For a while."

Chapter 2: Revelation, Redemption, and Retaliation

London England: Victor Frankenstein's Castle

The following morning, George, the captain, and Victor sat at the kitchen table eating beans and eggs with bread and sipping tea while George and the captain filled Victor in on the details of the last year of his life and what they had done to bring him back. Victor nodded a lot but never quit eating and never looked up at either of them. He let the absurd nature of the story sink in with each bite and then be washed away with each sip of tea. A knot had begun forming in his gut—or rather his creature's gut, which was now his own. He looked through eyes that had once belonged to his creature, the monster that had longed for acceptance and love, that had become so angry and vengeful. All the memories, the fragments, the watery moments all came together at once. He said, around a mouthful of bread, "Is that it? All of it?"

The captain dabbed his mouth with a napkin. "Aye, all of it. I, for one, am glad to have you back, Victor, and I hope you understand why I followed in your footsteps instead of turning all of this over to authorities."

Victor set the bent fork on the table. He stared at it for a moment. He was so much stronger, his hands so much larger. "I was trying to destroy the creature when I died." He peered up at the captain, tears welling in his eyes and a red flush coloring his cheeks.

"Well, his speaking is vastly improved overnight," George said to Victor.

The captain shot him a dirty look. "Not now, George." He pushed the plate aside. "Victor, I know that you wanted to end the experiment and end all the death the creature brought. It would be such a pity to science and the world to let a brilliant mind like yours go to waste. Besides, I missed you, mate."

Victor pushed his plate aside, and it slid across the table and tumbled to the floor. "Sorry," he said and pulled his teacup forward and cupped it between his two big hands. "My mind is in those writings… Rantings of a madman…the man I was. I should never have done what I did. Never. If I hadn't, no one would have died. I have to live with that all over again and without my…love."

"You didn't kill anyone, Victor," George said. "It was the brain. It was always the brain. It was defective. I improved your methods, and we used your brain." He picked up his plate and set it on the counter; his energy back on high. "Look at you! You're a miracle. And now you can share that brilliance with others. Think of the strides we could make in medic—"

"Enough!" Victor shouted and stood, knocking the chair backward, across the floor and into the far wall. "We will not be sharing this…this freak show," he gestured to himself, "with anyone. There will be no further…uh…studies! I'm an abomination, a freak—a horrific monster! Just like with my creature, people will fear me and run screaming. Authorities will hunt me. You don't realize what you've done!"

"Victor. It's not like that, mate. We—"

"There is no 'we.' There is only me. You'll see," Victor said and stomped from the room, nearly taking the door with him.

"Aye," said the captain. "He just needs some time."

Victor made his way upstairs to his room, tripping up the stairs and clunking down the hall. He hated how he had little control over this body—all his fine breeding, manners, and finesse gone. He knew this would abate in time as he acclimated to his new body, but he would never be the same. For years, he'd believed the man was his mind and the mind carried the body. Now, in this body, he wasn't so sure about his theories.

He stood in the room where his mirror had hung, now just a blank spot on the wall. He knew why the captain had removed it; he'd witnessed what happened when his creature, the man he was now, looked in that mirror all those years ago. Yet, he craved it. He needed to see his face in better detail than his hands or body could show. He hunted all over the room, under the bed, in the closets, behind the wardrobe and the dresser. He made his way to the bathing room, where he hoped to find a handheld glass used for shaving and grooming. No mirrors. As his frustration grew, he wondered if the creature's face would be different since he looked at it with his own eyes, if George and the captain had made alterations. He supposed they would not have; yet when he touched his face, felt the lines of stitches, he just couldn't determine if these were new or reopened or the same. His mind's eye saw the creature he'd chased across Europe and into the Arctic, across the ice and to the ship of the captain he'd befriended. The face haunted him more now than it had then. The thought sickened him and made his chest hurt. Who in their right mind would befriend him, respect him; what woman would ever want him? Tears stung his eyes, and he wiped them away. Is this the way the creature felt? *God help me.*

He hurried back downstairs, pounding the steps, losing his footing, catching himself, and found his way back to the kitchen. George and the captain weren't there. He stepped out of the room and shouted, "Captain? George?"

"We're in the lab," the captain yelled.

Victor groaned and made his way to the lab, nearly falling into the room off the bottom step. "Where are all my mirrors?"

George and the captain looked at each other.

"Do you think I don't know what I look like?" Victor pleaded. "One of the last things I saw on this earth was my creature's face. I made this face!" He glanced between the two men, whose mouths were agape. "Please. I need one of my full-length mirrors." Victor sat in the chair, and it groaned.

"I put the long ones in the icehouse," the captain said. "I just didn't want you to be shocked right away."

Victor sighed, a deep guttural noise. "Very well. I'll go there." He got up to leave.

"I can bring it back in for you if you want me to, mate," the captain said.

"Not necessary." Victor turned and headed up the stairs.

As Victor pushed through the kitchen pantry's door and into the cold, wet day, he stopped and watched the plumes of steam rise and dissipate with each breath. Nothing about the cold bothered him; he wasn't cold at all... *The cold doesn't affect me*...and yet everything about it did. Between him and the horizon, he saw nothing and no one, and this was something he'd cherished during his time as the madman creating a monster and now cherished for its ability to hide him away from the world.

When he entered the icehouse, it was as he'd left it, except the tables were gone. He looked around until he saw the covered mirrors stuffed behind an ice block. A tentative tug caused the cover to slip but not fall. He stopped—stood looking at the cover and his shaking hand upon it. He knew what he'd see, and his cheeks burned. Another yank and the cover fell. As it did, Victor averted his gaze to the floor and stepped back, a chill working its way up his spine.

Suddenly, his mouth was as dry as a summer desert, and he licked his lips, swallowed hard. He began at the base of the mirror and continued until his gaze fell upon the face that so terrified him. For a moment, he couldn't breathe. The anguished cry that left him didn't seem his own, and it sent him to his knees. Tears flowed freely, and he cried for every death he'd known; yet, his eyes could not turn from what he saw in the mirror. All he could see was the creature looking back; he saw no fragment of himself, not even in his eyes. He was trapped in his own creation, and he could not bear it but could not look away. After a few minutes, he pulled himself to his feet; his grief turned dark, rising into a rage he'd not known since the creature killed his fiancée. Punching and kicking, he shattered the mirror and the ones hidden with it until he had nothing left and lay flat on the icehouse floor. "What have you done, Captain..."

Victor awoke to a hand on his arm. The captain leaned over him.

"Victor, come in. You might not be able to feel the cold, but it certainly knows you."

"Why? Why did you bring me back to this misery? The woman I love is dead. My family is gone. My reputation ruined. And now, I am dead to everyone who knew me." The pain he felt now stung more than he thought it should. He realized how cold he'd been to his creation and how much the creature had wanted acceptance and love, neither of which he nor anyone had been willing to give.

"You're not dead, Victor. The body doesn't make the man; the mind makes the man. Your words. And you are here with me."

Victor sat up. "Be that as it may, you didn't answer my question."

"It was somewhat a selfish deed, mate. I wanted my friend back, the man that told the most brilliant stories of science and discovery. I also did it for science, so you could go on and discover more."

Victor wondered if any of that was true. He wondered if the captain had merely fallen prey, become intoxicated with the idea of reanimation as he had. "Perhaps you and George should have just stepped into my shoes and left me out of it, used some other brain for this madness."

"That would've just created more madness, Victor. The idea was to bring you back. To show the world that, with the right brain, the reanimation process might offer a means of saving loved ones or a means to keep great minds alive or even a path to everlasting life. And," he said more seriously, "it wouldn't have been you, mate."

Victor stood on wobbly legs, his hand on the wall. "No man should live forever; it's not natural. What we've created, dear Captain, is a route no man should take. Knowledge is passed from one generation to the next. Nature fixes itself, rights its wrongs. It will do the same here."

The captain stood. "George is leaving, going back to Cambridge in the morning. He has agreed not to write of his findings or discuss what's happened here until I give him the go-ahead. We'll figure this out, you and me, mate. Now, come in because even if you're not freezing, I am."

The captain and Victor went into the kitchen, where George sat by the warmth of the woodstove, making tea.

"You all right, Victor?" George asked.

"For now," Victor said. "I hear you're going back to Cambridge in the morning."

"My, your voice is spot on, and you're moving better," George said, setting teacups on the table and filling them.

"This is the Victor I remember," said the captain. "A man of stories and conversation."

"Except I'm not the Victor you knew, Captain, and I can never be him again. I am a man without a place in an empty world that will despise me—a man no family would have, that no woman could ever love."

That poor creature…so alone… We are together at long last, forever together. You will never be alone again. At least I have the captain… I'm sorry that I was not your Captain…

The captain, whose cup had been at his lips, set it on the table. "Victor, you most certainly are the same man. Your body is different but no different than if you'd been in battle or run over by a carriage. You are still you, mate, and we will sail again. You will have more stories to tell, more adventures to take. You will find a woman, and I have some ideas about that, too."

"Will you, by chance, need a doctor on those voyages?" George asked.

"Why? Are you interested in gaining your sea legs?" the captain asked.

"If it's with you and Victor, oh, yes indeed, I would. I would set sail this very moment!" George said, his eyes sparkling.

"Well, then… Perhaps more schooling just isn't in the cards for you after all, George," the captain said.

"I think I'll go finish this year. I'm sure you won't be up to travel for some time yet. The more I learn, the more I can be of service to you both," George said.

"So be it," the captain said. "What do you think, Victor?"

Victor pushed his teacup aside, and it fell to the floor. He looked at the mess and then gazed at the two men seated across from him. "You two just don't see it, do you? We'll never set sail. We'll never leave this castle. The authorities will find something…some tidbit of information that will send them running with torches to find us."

"Not this time, Victor. No one knows you're alive outside this room. The harbormaster, that man who spreads rumors with such ease, is right now spreading the rumor that I'm here on your bequest awaiting your arrival, which will never come, of course. No one will suspect anything," the captain said and pushed the chair out. "You've been given an extraordinary gift, a rare chance, Victor. You can seek redemption in new pursuits, put right what your creature made wrong. Not many souls have chances such as those, mate."

Even if he sought the redemption the captain spoke of, Victor knew the good people of London and the authorities would find out and seek not redemption for their actions against him and the creature, but retaliation for the creature's actions and on him for creating such an abomination in the first place, and now the captain and George would be pulled into the mess. "We'll see," he said.

Chapter 3: A Letter from George

London, England: Victor's Frankenstein's Castle

Over the weeks that followed George's return to Cambridge, Victor and the captain fell into a comfortable routine. The captain planned their next sea adventure to Brazil and did the marketing, and Victor, though his voice, memory, and movement continued to improve, fell deeper into a well of depression and anger. The captain made a point of going into town for groceries and to spread the word of his life at Victor Frankenstein's castle. He collected any post and often ate at a local inn, where he was quick to make friends and learn of any news from authorities.

One afternoon, the captain returned from such an outing with a newspaper and some letters. He stood at the kitchen table, where Victor sat sulking over his tea.

"We've post today, Victor," the captain said. "A letter from

George." He laid the letter on the table along with a bundle of fresh fish wrapped in paper and tied with a loaf of fresh bread on top and pulled a newspaper from inside his coat. "Here, I brought you the paper. I haven't read it yet." He scooted the newspaper across the table until the edge poked Victor's arm. He took off his coat and tossed it over the back of the chair and sat. "Oh, and I got some very nice fish from the harbor today. I thought we could have it for dinner."

Victor didn't look up. "I don't want the paper. I don't want fish." He banged his fists on the table, and he said, "I'd like the company of a woman."

"I see." He said and poured some tea into a cup. "That might be a bit tricky."

"I want a woman's company. A prostitute would be fine. It's just for a night. I recall a brothel near the harbor."

The captain sipped his tea, never taking his eyes off Victor. "You realize no one can see you, right? You still look like the monster the authorities are after."

"Yes, yes, I know. Just bring her here. Perhaps you could blind-fold her so she doesn't know where she's going or who she's with. She'd be none the wiser for the trip."

"Right, blindfold a prostitute." He sipped more tea, his eyes brightening. "I suppose that could work. There's plenty of women at the wharf looking for money; I'll just hire one of them."

"Just pay her well; she'll come," Victor said and decided that maybe he would read the newspaper after all.

"Alright, mate. I'll go back to town and see what I can find." He picked up the letter and opened it, his face growing first slack and then tense.

"What is it, Captain? Has something happened to George?"

"We've got a problem, Victor," the captain said, pushing the letter toward Victor.

September 13, 1816

Dearest Captain,

The weather remains terribly cold here in Cambridge. Yesterday we had a freeze! Imagine that. A freeze in September! Papers tell of the crops failing and people dying from cold and hunger all over the continent, as if that wasn't a big issue already, so on that news, I hope you both are faring well.

This letter finds me well but worried as events have turned against our favor. Today, I write with a heavy heart and with some news concerning Dr. Roberson. I know he was your friend and ally, so this may come as a bit of a shock. He was found dead in his chemistry lab the very day we left for Victor's castle. It was quite a horrific end from what I gather. The point is that the authorities came to the university and questioned all the students, including me. I told them I'd been away when the murder occurred. I don't know to what extent they will push me to tell them where I was or who I was with. So far, I've said nothing, and they have moved on to other witnesses. There is a chance, though, that other students will remember your attendance at the class the day before the murder, and I thought you should be prepared for authorities to arrive for questioning. I hope I'm wrong on that account.

Write me soon, as I anxiously await news.

Faithfully yours, George

"That is a problem," Victor said. "What if he cracks and tells them everything? What if the authorities do come out here?"

"They won't," the captain said. "I'm going to visit Cambridge again and make myself available for questioning. I'll be cooperative, and they won't suspect anything, I promise. I'll leave first thing in the morning."

"That should work nicely. Besides, you'll need to take the prostitute back to town. You can do that on the way."

"Except it's not on the way. I'll just pay her to stay one more night."

"Sounds perfect to me," Victor said. "The paper mentions the murder of that professor. All it says is that authorities are investigating."

"That's to be expected, Victor. I'll take care of this, and you can enjoy your female companionship. I'm going to put these fish in the icehouse and head out. I should be back in a few hours," the captain said and put his coat back on.

Victor set the paper aside and thought about the warmth of a woman. He missed that almost more than anything else. He watched from the kitchen window as the captain rode away on his horse.

Chapter 4: The Monster Reborn

London, England: Frankenstein's Castle

That evening, the captain led the blindfolded woman into the kitchen, where he sat her down across from Victor. Victor noted her long, dark hair was piled in a loose bun, with stray strands dangling against her face and neck. She wore a blue coat over a blue dress and boots on her feet, and she sat in a manner that showed her ankles, which he rather admired. The simple, white cloth blindfold hid her eyes, but her mouth, smudged with a bit of rouge, smiled.

"Give her some tea," Victor said to the captain. "She must be cold."

"Victor, this is Lilith," the captain said, pouring Lilith some tea. "How do you take your tea, Lilith?"

Lilith's voice was as smooth and soft as silk. "One sugar and hint of cream."

The captain handed her the cup, and she sipped.

"Thank you," she said.

"You're quite welcome, love. I'll be in my room if you need any-thing, Victor," the captain said and left the room.

"So, Lilith, have you ever been in a castle before?" Victor asked.

"A time or two," she said. "Is this your castle, Victor?"

"It is." He drank some of his tea. "Uh, do you like big men?"

"The bigger, the better."

"I'm glad to hear that because I'm very large," he said and sipped his tea. Her smile was contagious, and each time she shifted in the chair and he caught a glimpse of her legs, something deep inside him stirred. He cleared his throat. "Listen, and this is important, Lilith. Under no circumstances should you remove your blindfold during your stay here. Do you understand?"

"The captain explained everything to me before we left the har-bor, Victor. It's all clear."

"Good. I'm glad that's out of the way so we can enjoy ourselves."

"What would you like, Victor," she asked.

"I'd like your company, Lilith, in every way imaginable."

She smiled again and pushed the cup aside. She stood and felt her way around the table until she reached his arm. "Your arm is so very big. I like that."

Victor stood. "Let's go upstairs to my room. I've started a nice fire, and there's a pot of tea, or, if you'd like, I have whiskey or brandy."

"Brandy would be nice," she said.

Victor led her to his room and sat her in one of the chairs near the fire. He sat in a chair next to her and poured two snifters of brandy and handed one to her, placing it into her hand. "Does the fire suit you?"

"Oh, it's lovely." She sipped the brandy. "And this is quite nice, too."

"I'm glad you approve," Victor said and swallowed his brandy, then refilled the snifter.

"So, what's your story, Victor, that you needed me here in a castle blindfolded?"

Victor was glad she couldn't see him squirm. "Could you come sit by me on the bed?"

"That'd be nice, Victor." She stood.

Victor guided her to the bed, and they sat on the edge. "I've got a confession to make," he said. "I'm more than just a big man, Lilith. I-I have certain…shall we say…deformities that I want to make you aware of. They might feel strange to you, and I wanted to warn you about them before we begin."

Lilith shifted closer to Victor and reached out until her hand came into contact with his chest. She turned toward him. "It's okay, love. I've seen all types. I'd really like to help you feel better, to feel wanted. May I touch you?"

Victor felt a chill race up his spine and butterflies rush around in his stomach. His heartbeat sped up, and he could feel sweat prickling his brow. "I want you to," he said.

Slowly, Lilith worked her way around his chest and arms, then up to his shoulders, and then to his neck.

Victor put his hands over hers. "You might not like what you feel," he said. "Are you sure you want to go on? I can have the captain—"

She slid her hand to his mouth. "I'm fine, Victor. I want to touch you." She went back to his neck and moved her body closer to his.

Lilith radiated heat, and when she moved closer, a lust began to stir such as he hadn't felt since his first bedding with his bride to be. His breathing quickened, and her touch made him moan, a guttural growling that he had no control over.

Lilith searched his neck, and her fingers ran over the cuts and stitches. When she reached his face, her fingers traced the outline of his face. Each time she felt a cut or a stitch, she spent more time touching, caressing.

Her face was inches from his, and he felt her warm, sweet breath on his mouth. Then she kissed him, leaning into it, putting her hands on the sides of his cheeks. He felt her body brush his, and something more awakened. He threw his arms around her and flipped her onto her back, a maneuver that surprised even him. He clawed at her clothing, and she helped him help her out of her dress and petty coats. Next, he clawed at her corset and became frustrated when it wouldn't give.

"If you back up, love, I can undress, and you can, too," she said.

He rolled away, pulled off his shirt, and awkwardly shook off his pants. When he looked at her again, she was naked, lying on her back. She fumbled for his hand and guided him back. She kissed him, and he pushed against her harder. She moaned…

And then she suddenly screamed. "What are you?"

He peered down, still caught in the heat and the frenzy; her blindfold had slipped to her chin, and she was staring at him with wide, fear-filled eyes, tears welling. He fell to his elbows.

She struggled beneath him. "*Get. Off. Of. Me!* Get off! Help! Somebody help me!" she screamed.

He put a hand over her mouth and leaned close. "Please, stop screaming," he demanded through clenched teeth.

Lilith squirmed under him, scratching, bucking, and making squealing noises. He tightened his grip over her mouth. "Quite now," he said.

Her eyes became impossibly big—the whites reddening, tears spilling; she fought and scratched even harder, her legs drumming the bed. He tightened his grip again, digging into the soft flesh of her cheeks—across her mouth, against her nose…

Such beautiful brown eyes…so warm…so soft…he needed her…

When he'd finished and regained some semblance of himself, he peeled his hand away from her mouth. She no longer struggled. Her lips were parted, and a tiny dribble of blood trickled from the corner and down her chin.

"Lilith?" He shook her. "Lilith? … No… *No… No… please, no!*"

Victor rolled off the bed and ran from the room and down the hall to the captain's room. He flung the door open, nearly pulling it from its hinges.

The captain sat in a chair, tea in hand, a chart laid before him on a table. His eyes widened.

"Captain! Come quick. Something's wrong with Lilith!"

The captain set the cup down and hurried behind Victor to his room. He stopped just inside the door, and his stomach knotted. On the bed, he saw Lilith. She wasn't moving, and her chest didn't rise and fall. He hurried to the bed and put his head to her chest. He could hear no heartbeat; his ear near her mouth felt no breath. Her lips had a blue tinge under the smeared rouge. Her brown eyes were the size of saucers and wide open, but there was no life in them. He turned to Victor. "What happened?"

"I-I'm not sure. I think I might have accidentally suffocated her…" He stared at his hands. "Her blindfold fell off, and she screamed… I just wanted her to stop screaming…"

The captain's head dropped forward, and he put a hand to his forehead. "That you did, mate. That you did." He took a deep breath and looked up at Victor. "What's done is done." He stood. "And put some clothes on. We need to get rid of her body, preferably some-place far from here."

The captain redressed Lilith, and Victor helped him wrap the body in a sheet, carry it to the barn, and lay it over the back of the captain's horse.

"I'll be back in a couple of hours," the captain said. "Best not to wait up for me."

Victor nodded. The worst had happened, and it was this monster's body, the very body that had murdered so many, that had now murdered Lilith. So, it's not the brain alone that makes the monster. It's the process that makes the monster—the body, the chemicals, the reanimation… *Oh, Captain, if only you'd known what I know and ended this madness.* Yet, some part of him wanted to live, wanted to be loved and accepted…like the creature he'd scorned. If only her blindfold hadn't slipped…if only…

The next morning at breakfast, neither man discussed Lilith, and both ate in silence.

When the captain set out for Cambridge, Victor watched him ride away and said, "I want a woman I can keep."

Chapter 5: Lonesome

London, England: Frankenstein's Castle

When the captain returned to the castle, Victor was still sitting at the kitchen table with his head hung low.

"Everything, okay, mate?"

Victor looked up. "In some ways, I suppose… You are, after all, a good friend, something I wasn't for the creature I created… I wish my heart had been as kind as yours."

The captain laid his coat over the chair, poured some tea, and sat. "You did the best you could given the situation of that creature's mind."

"No, I don't think I did. You, on the other hand, Captain, you be-friended me, protected me." He bit into a biscuit. "After what hap-pened, I knew I didn't want to be the creature I created or the man I was when I created him. Listen, I thought about how to prevent an-other Lilith."

"And that would be?"

"There is only one way I can be with anyone other than you. That someone must be sightless. I need a woman who can't see me and who doesn't need to be blindfolded… Someone I can be with for what's left of this miserable life, someone who can make me happy beyond our friendship and that perhaps I can make happy."

"I will try, my friend," the captain said. "I will try."

Chapter 6: Frankenstein Isn't the Only Monster

Cambridge, England: Cambridge University Medical Facility

When the captain arrived at the medical facility, he witnessed no authorities at or around the entrance, no horses or buggies. He tied his horse to a tree and went inside the lobby. Miss Jackson sat her desk, but gone was the cheery smile.

"Miss Jackson?"

"Ah, Captain. It's good to see you," she said, managing a weak smile.

"I heard about Doctor Roberson. I'm so sorry."

The slight smile faded and her face crinkled, seeming to fold in on itself. She began to cry. "He was killed right here in his classroom in a horrible and unspeakable manner. The poor man lay there in his chemistry room for hours before a young student found his body."

The captain handed her a handkerchief. "Again, my condolences on his untimely passing. Are the authorities still on the grounds?"

"No, Captain. They finished up here over a week ago," she said, dabbing her eyes with a handkerchief. "They talked to everyone for days, all the students, me, the other professors, the people around campus. They never said anything, but after a few days, it was over. When I asked about the murder and the investigation, one constable told me he'd be in touch, and that if I thought of anything, I should visit the station." She handed the handkerchief.

Stuffing the used handkerchief in his jacket pocket by its ends, he said, "I see. Where might that station be?"

"It's down the road from the inn, just past the bridge. Why do you ask?"

"I'd like to help, if I can. I was here the day before. Maybe something I saw could help."

"That's right kind of you, Captain. I'm sure they'll be glad to see you."

"I met a student here by the name of…uh…Kensington, I believe. Would he be in class today?"

"Oh, yes. Doctor Kensington would be in the lab right now. Class under the new professor should be finishing up about now."

"Thank you, Miss Jackson."

The captain made his way to the dungeon-like classroom and laboratory just as the class was letting out. He spotted George and waved him over.

"I'm glad to see you're okay, Captain, but isn't it dangerous you being here?"

"Not at all, George. It's part of my plan. Walk with me."

As the two men made their way to the exit, the captain said, "I'm going to see the authorities about the murder. As you noted, I was here the day before and the day of, so it's best if I just go give them a statement and clear my name…and yours. Afterward, the authorities will have no purpose in revisiting you because I will have distracted them."

George stopped on the last step. "Oh, that's good news. What do you mean distracted?"

"Don't worry about it, mate. I've got it handled. In the meantime, you need to stay quiet about what we've learned, you know, about Victor. Don't write anything or say anything to anyone. Leave any notes you've written with me. I'll keep them safe until we meet next. Hopefully, we'll have everything for our trip worked out by then, and you'll be done with classes. It will be during that voyage that we can decide what to write and who to write it to."

"All right. I just know the scientific and medical communities here at the university would just be mesmerized by the knowledge of Victor and what it could mean."

"I'm sure, mate, but you cannot speak of it right now."

"I won't. I promise," George said. "How will I know when you're ready to move on this?"

"I'll come get you. It's probably best that we aren't seen together, at least until I'm sure it's safe."

George studied him, and that made the captain uncomfortable for the first time since meeting him. "Everything okay, mate?"

"Yes, of course. It's just hard to keep a secret of this magnitude when it could mean so much to so many."

Or it could make you out to be a madman and get us hung, the captain thought.

"Very, well, then George. One last thing."

"Yes."

"You know a lot of people in town. Are there any young ladies who are blind?"

George smiled. "There is a blind fortune teller at the docks. She is very winsome, too."

The captain thought about it for a moment. He tipped his hat. "Until we meet again."

George did the same and meandered away. The farther George walked into the distance, the more the captain's regret grew. He turned, mounted his horse, and headed to the station.

At the station, the captain met with the lead detective on the Roberson case. He told him about meeting Dr. Roberson and coming to visit him at his class. He told him about a young man who was secretive and who carried a knife.

"So, you met Doctor Roberson to gather information about chemistry for your sailors." He consulted his notes. "To keep them safe on your next voyage?" the detective asked.

"Yes, exactly. Doctor Roberson was helpful. He lent me a book on plants, which I returned the next morning. When I saw him last, he was with a student, a young man with dark hair… George, I think his name was."

"Very good, then, sir. I appreciate you bringing this to our attention." The detective stood and thrust out his hand.

The captain shook it. "Anything I can do to help."

"Right. If you think of anything else, send word."

The captain nodded and left. He had some time to burn, so he decided to eat at the inn, where he made sure he was seen, though he elected not to strike up any conversations as he ate. Luckily for him, Miss Harrow was elsewhere when he arrived.

On the way back to the castle that evening, the captain made a detour to the flat on the university grounds where George resided. He entered through an open window. George slept on the couch with a book perched like a tent on his chest. The captain planted a bloodstained knife of the same type he'd stabbed Dr. Roberson with, along with a few choice pages of George's rantings about reanimation. He snuck back to the window, stopping to watch George for a moment longer. "Sorry, mate. You left me no choice."

Outside, he walked his horse for a block, then mounted and headed toward the castle.

Chapter 7: Love is Blind

London, England: Frankenstein's Castle

The captain rushed back into the castle and saw Victor sitting by the crackling fireplace. "Well, then mate, you may be in luck."

"What?" Victor turned from watching the fire and looked at the captain.

"When I was in the market, I chanced upon a woman selling bread. The smell of fresh bread was intoxicating, so I thought I'd bring some home to have with the fish. Behind her wares table was a wagon, and I noticed a sign painted on the side that read 'Fortunes by Rosella Black-thorn—Runes Reading.' We struck up a conversation, and she told me her husband and young son had died in a storm while fishing. She told me she read runes for a penny, and I told her maybe next time. She smiled then, and it was quite warm, and her blue eyes were quite bright, but it wasn't until I asked her for the round bread that I noticed she was blind." The captain sipped the tea. He could still smell the bread…

* * *

The petite woman, wearing a colorful dress and a bright scarf on her head to cover her long, dark hair, reached into a basket with delicate fingers that felt their way around the loaves.

"Is this one you wanted, kind sir?" she asked.

"It's perfect, lass," the captain said, still staring at her unique beauty. "I hope this isn't too forward, but do you mind if I ask how long you've been blind?"

She laughed. "Of course not. Happens all the time. I was born without sight, so I'm really not missing anything. My world is a kitchen filled with aromas, sounds, and tastes. My imagination tells me all about the things I can't see, sir."

"That's much the way the world is, lass. Sight sometimes skews the real from the fantastic."

"You smell of salt and fish," she said and laughed.

"I imagine I do. I so happen to have some fish in a package. I'm the captain, and my fate in life is to sail the seas and explore."

"I envy you, Captain. The freedom of the sea, the wind at your back. I should like to try that one day," she said, her unseeing eyes sparkling at something only she understood. "I'll just wrap it for you." She felt along the edge of the table to some brown paper and wrapped it, tying it with string. She handed it to him. "That'll be two pence."

The captain dug in his lapel pocket. "What's your name, lass?"

"I'm Rosella, but my friends just call me Rose."

He handed her the money. "It's been a pleasure, Rose. I hope to visit with you again soon. Are you in the market every day?"

"Not always, but most days," she said.

"Well, good day to you, Rose."

"Good day to you, Captain, and I do hope to see you again."

"Oh, I'm sure you will, Rose," the captain said and walked away into the crowded market…

"Even at that moment, after I met Rose, I thought of you, Victor. Our luck couldn't't've been better," the captain said.

Victor stared across the table. The captain's gaze was not on him, and he realized it was in the moment, reliving the story as he told it. "Do you think this Rose could be interested in me?"

The captain blinked and cleared his throat. "Perhaps."

The next evening, when the captain arrived home from the market, Rose was with him. He led her to the kitchen and helped her to a seat. He leaned close to Victor's ear. "I've made an arrangement with Rose. I paid her a handsome some that will set her for life should anything go wrong with our plans, mate. In return, she's agreed to be your wife and companion. She told me that she'd have done it for nothing but the companionship and care of a man. I still insisted there be a contract. She agreed." He stood and looked down at Victor. Victor nodded his agreement. "Victor, this is Rose. Rose, Victor," the captain said. "I'll leave you two to get acquainted and see to dinner."

"Good evening, Victor. It's nice to make your acquaintance," Rose said.

"The pleasure is mine," Victor said. He came around the table and took her hand. He kissed it. "Care for tea? Something stronger?"

"Tea would be nice," she said, standing to shrug out of her coat.

The captain had been right. She was a raw beauty, like a diamond buried in a mine, and her blue eyes were indeed crystal clear, though they looked at something beyond him. He poured her tea and pushed the cream and sugar within her reach. "Did the captain explain my situation?"

"He did, and I'm terribly sorry for your troubles. I've troubles of my own, too, you see. I've been widowed and childless these last two years, and times are hard." She squeezed his hand. "I hope things will be best if we work them out together," she said, reaching to touch him.

Victor stepped back; her pain was all too familiar to him. He wasn't ready to let her touch him. "You should want for nothing, Rose. All I ask is that you stay by my side and comfort me."

"We all need comfort. We both have issues that push people away. I promise I won't push you away."

Her words were soft and her look sincere. Victor wanted to believe, needed to believe love was possible. "I'm glad for the arrangement," he said.

The captain cleared his throat. He was standing in the doorway and motioned for Victor to join him.

"Excuse me a moment, would you? I think the captain would like a word."

"Of course," she said.

Victor joined the captain in the hall.

"Now that she's settled a bit, I wanted to tell you that I'm moving up the trip to Brazil. I made all the arrangements while I was at the harbor this morning. It appears that George spilled the beans when confronted with the murder of his professor, and the authorities want to speak with me again, here, day after next. I don't trust they won't be earlier."

"That is troubling, but I'm glad you handled it. Did you take care of our singing canary?" Victor asked.

The captain turned away. "I couldn't bring myself to kill him, and I don't think we can take him with us either. He doesn't know what really happened and that's for the best. It's a risk, aye; he knows where we planned to go, but now that the cat's out of the bag, we must go, start over in Brazil like we've been planning. I've hired the least number of sailors to help with the voyage, a ratty lot, but they're no friends of the authorities."

"George already talked, so at this point, maybe his death wouldn't change anything. It seems it's my fate to be discovered." Victor sipped the tea, but something scratched at the back of his mind. *Was fate indeed intervening in this unnatural situation to thwart his happiness and peace like it had for his creature?* He said, "Was Rose in agreement with the trip?"

"She was. She said she had nothing holding here, that she could conduct her business anywhere." He glanced at Victor. "We'll set sail tomorrow evening. I'll pack as much as I can into the carts. I suggest you pack what you really want because we're never coming back."

"All right. I believe, as I have since you first spoke of it, that this is the best move we have. I hear Brazil has a booming gold and diamond mining industry."

"Aye, they do. I've a friend who can help us. I sent a courier via ship ahead of us to let him know we're coming. I venture the letter will arrive about two days before we do," the captain said.

"I hope that is a promise you don't end up breaking, Captain. Bad luck follows the creature wherever it goes, and it will be no different for me."

"Bullocks. You might be in your creation's body, but you are not your creation. We'll be fine, and we'll prosper. We will travel the seas again, you and me, Victor. You'll see."

"Perhaps." Victor walked back into the kitchen and sat, fidgeting with the teacup.

"Is everything okay, Victor?" Rose asked.

"Of course, yes, but we've decided to journey to Brazil sooner than anticipated. Does that suit you?"

Her eyes sparkled. "Oh, yes. I've always wanted to travel."

Victor returned with the fish and potatoes he'd cooked on the woodstove, along with the warmed round bread. As they ate and made conversation, Victor, in that moment, forgot that he was a monster.

After dinner, the captain excused himself to continue packing, while Victor and Rose retired to his room. Some of her bags sat by the chairs in front of the fire, and Victor realized that the captain had not brought all her belongings into the castle. It seemed he was planning to take both carts.

"Please, sit," Victor said.

Rose took a seat and warmed herself.

"Are you nervous about being with me?" he asked.

"To be with you? No," she said.

"But?" he asked.

"But I want to know you before we…"

"Indeed. We shall then get to know one another. Come sit with me on the bed."

"All right," she said, but made no move to rise.

Victor stood intent on getting over to the bed. He walked toward her chair, then stopped. He peered at the bed, and the memories of Lilith flooded back. "Never mind," he said. She looked uncomfortable. "Let's just sit, have tea, and talk."

Rose brightened. "Perfect," she said.

Before Victor sat, he moved his chair close to hers. "Is this all right?"

Rose reached and touched first the chair and then his arm. "Perfect," she said and gave his arm a gentle squeeze before moving her hand to his.

For some hours, they talked and laughed, and Victor's gloom began to lift. She was everything he'd wanted her to be—kind, friendly, warm, and a good conversationalist.

"What do you look like, Victor?" she asked.

And just like that, the dark cloud reformed above his head, and his heart sank. "I have dark hair with a tinge of gray and green eyes. I'm a big man with some…well…" He looked over at her, his tongue tied. He realized he was describing what he once looked like. "Maybe you should find out for yourself," he said.

She stood and felt her way to his chair. She found his knees and laid one hand on his arm and reached with the other across his body. "You're quite wide, too," she said and laughed. Her fingers found his shoulders, and she leaned closer to him. "May I sit?"

"Be my guest," he said.

She sat on his knee. He could smell honeysuckle and flowers; he could feel the heat of her body near his. His heart sped up as her fingers made their way up his chest to his neck, where they stopped on one of the scars.

"Were you injured?" she asked.

"Quite grievously," he said. "An accident."

"I'm so sorry. That must've been hard for you," she said, moving fingers from his neck to his jaw.

A trail of heat laid in the wake of her fingers as they traced the features of his face, touching every point, each line, each dip, feeling each stitch, each scar. Her fingers ran across his nose and over his eyes, then played with his ears. The desire inside him heated up, and he wanted nothing more than to hold her, to have her. His breaths were short and hard, almost a pant, increasing with her every touch. Victor took her hands in his. "Please," he said. "It's too much."

She kissed the side of his mouth, and it felt like the kiss of the summer morning sun. "I—"

Rose placed her fingers over his lips. "Shhh. You're wonderful, Victor, beautiful and perfect in every way."

He kissed her then, his arms pulling her to him…and the world melted away.

Chapter 8: Voyage to Brazil

London, England: Port of London

By early the next afternoon, Victor and the captain had packed all they wished to take onto the two carts and covered the remaining furniture and equipment in the castle. All the fires were out, and the castle somehow felt more than just abandoned when they walked through the front doors for the last time.

Victor stood staring at his home, the place where all this mess had begun, and he wondered what life would have been like had he listened to the warnings of friends and colleagues and had never gone through with creating the creature. No matter how he tried, though, he couldn't picture it—not his family, not his fiancée, not a life beyond this one. He pulled the keys and the deed to the castle from his pocket and turned to Rose. "I want you to have these in case anything ever happens to me."

She looked up at Victor. "Nothing will happen. Fate is on our side, Victor. We'll be fine in Brazil. We'll get a new castle and a new lab so you can continue your work," she said.

"Please, just take them and keep them safe," he said, closing her hand around the items. He helped her into the wagon, climbed up on the other side, and snapped the reins. The wagon pulled away, with the captain close behind with an equally laden cart.

By the time they reached the harbor, the sun had set. They pulled the carts close to the ramp. The sailors the captain had hired unloaded these onto the ship. The captain then sold the carts and horses to two gentlemen he'd met earlier that day.

They boarded, and within the hour, the ship was bound for Brazil.

Chapter 9: The Beginning of the End

United Kingdom of Portugal: Port of Brazil

The trip took nearly a week, but the weather had been on their side, and it had been smooth sailing the entire way; as they sailed farther south, it got warmer. One gorgeous evening, three days into the voyage at sunset, the captain married Victor and Rose, as was his right and duty at sea. Victor thought maybe Rose had been right and fate was on their side, but something dark still lurked in the back of his mind, pulling on what happiness he could muster.

When they arrived at the port in Brazil two days later, Victor paid the harbormaster, declared nothing, and, for small fee, moved straight though their cargo inspections. On his way out of the warehouse, the captain thought he saw a young man who looked exactly like George, but the man disappeared into the crowd. The captain shook his head. *It's probably just nerves*, he thought.

As he approached the end of the dock, the captain noted a good-sized cart with two horses. A driver stood beside it with a sign that read, "Captain & Company."

He approached the driver. "Good day. Are you José's driver?"

The driver stared questioningly at him. "José, sim."

The captain shrugged. "Do you speak any English?"

The driver shook his head. "Sem ingles, senhor. Portuguese."

The captain pointed at the sign and then himself.

The driver smiled. "Sim! Senhor José."

"Good." He pointed to his friends and the sailors moving cargo down the ramp and then pointed at the cart.

The driver nodded and laughed. "Sim, sim!"

The captain decided "sim" meant yes, so he motioned for Victor and Rose to join.

Victor approached, his dark cloak covering his mass and the hood pull partly over his face. Rose walked with her arm hooked in his.

"Do either of you speak Portuguese?" the captain asked.

"I do," Rose said. "It's a perk of being a fortune teller."

The captain eyed her but relented. He told her what to ask and say, and she relayed between the driver and the captain and crew. Soon, after the cart was packed and the sailors paid, they were on their way see José at Marscape Castle.

As they rode, the captain nudged Victor. "I saw a man that looked like George on the docks earlier. I'm sure I was mistaken, but…"

"I'm sure it was nothing," Rose said. "How could get here before us? Wasn't he the one at Cambridge?"

"He was when I last heard anything of him," the captain said. "Unless he took a ship that left at the same time I sent the letter to José, I don't see how he could be here."

"Do you think that's possible? After all, he did know where we were heading, and even if he didn't know all the facts, he always seemed to worry about our welfare," Victor said.

"Aye, true. He did seem excited. Besides, I'm sure even if he did manage to get here somehow, he would likely join us, not turn us in," the captain said.

"I've met George before. He would buy bread now and again… Nice man, and smart, too," Rose said. "I doubt he'd be any trouble."

The captain glanced at her sideways, a little voice telling him something didn't feel right. He ignored it. After all, he realized how protective he could be over Victor…and he might also be a tad jealous of the love Victor had found—the blind woman and the monster. Still, he said, "You never mentioned that before."

"Why would I? The subject never came up until now," she said.

"Just about everyone knows everyone else at Cambridge. Leave it be. She's probably right in any event," Victor said.

Victor now protected his wife, and that was as it should be, he supposed. "I doubt it was him anyway," the captain said, settling in his seat and crossing his arms. "He was being held at the station last I heard."

They rode in silence the rest of the way to the castle.

Chapter 10: The Accidental Incident

Brazil: Marscape Castle

Marscape Castle stood atop a cliffside overlooking the ocean. As the cart rounded the long, curving road with a steep incline, Victor cringed. The central part of the castle seemed to be in acceptable condition, but the east wing melted away into piles of crumbling wall and mounds of rubble. The west side fared marginally better, though a bit further along, the wall was crumbling, the last portion nothing more than large pieces of brick and stone. As they got closer, Victor noticed the stables were in good condition—for that he was grateful—and the wall around the property seemed to stretch as far as the eye could see both east and west. North was behind the castle, but he caught glimpses of the cliff's ragged edge. The salty smell of the ocean air felt familiar and inviting. If it had nothing else, he did like that it was by the sea, and he knew the captain would be spending hours looking out over the cliff's edge at the water. His money, his castle. It explained a lot as far as Victor was concerned. The castle needed repairs, and it was perched overlooking the sea. What more could the captain hope for in a home short of being at sea? Victor smiled. His friend would be happy, too.

As they pulled up to the gate, the driver pulled the reins, easing the horses to a stop, José Rivera, a round, dwarfish man with olive skin and a shiny bald head bounded through the gate leading from the inner courtyard.

"Welcome, welcome, senhors! Welcome, Captain!" he yelled, his accent thick.

The captain got off the cart and stretched. "Good to see you, mate." He looked around. "This is the best my money could buy?"

"I'm afraid so, unless you would like a tiny cottage in town on a plot of dirt. You ordered a castle, and here it is. You should be thankful. Most castles in this area are twice as big and occupied." José thrust his hand out.

The captain shook it. "It has a basement level, I gather."

"Of course, as you requested." He turned and said something in Portuguese to the driver. The driver popped the reins and the horses turned. The cart headed toward the barn. "Come in, come in. It's much better inside, I promise."

"I'm sure it must be," the captain said. "José, this is Victor and Rose."

He hurried over to them, shook Victor's hand with vigor, and kissed Rose's. "This way, this way."

José closed the gate behind them and led them across a barren courtyard, which must have once been the pride of the previous owner. For a moment, Victor could visualize how they must've amazed guests… Now, though, they lay in ruins—empty flower beds filled with weeds, dilapidated benches, broken picket fences, piles of uneven rubble where walls once graced the walkways, and pots with dead plants dotted each square.

Victor shook his head. "Such a shame, this yard."

"Well, my friend," José said, "You can fix it up all you'd like. It yours now."

José opened the main doors, and three women and one man filed out and stood on the walkway. He spoke to them in Portuguese, and they hurried across the courtyard, presumably to help bring their belongings inside.

Inside wasn't as bad as the outside had been. It was clean but sparsely furnished—a few tapestries and some mirrors hung on the walls, a long bench sat near a wall by a table, and a rusted suit of armor stood by the main stairway. Stained glass windows with sills big enough to sit on graced the main floor. Both were wide open. Victor looked up. Another window above was also open, allowing in an ocean breeze. He though this good architecture because it created a nice airflow that the thick walls helped cool. Unlike England, Brazil was hot and humid—

jungle-like.

"The staff will take your things to your rooms and move the crates to where you have indicated. So, for now, come to the kitchen. Maria has prepared a meal for us. I brought the drink." He smiled.

"No tea, eh?" the captain asked.

"Only if you brought it. We have coffee, though, if you'd like to try that."

"Coffee is fine," the captain said. He turned to Victor. "Don't worry. I brought a supply of English tea that should last you into the next century."

Victor smiled. "I should hope so. Coffee, indeed."

Over the months that followed, Victor and Rose began to settle into married life, and it was better than Victor could have ever dreamed. José visited now and again, and sometimes the captain traveled with him. The courtyard was on the mend, and the castle was fast becoming a home. Victor's fear of being seen decreased with each day that nothing happened, but he still wore his hooded cloak if he dared leave the castle. Most of the time, the captain, now lodged in the west wing, took Rose to do the marketing and run errands. Rose made it her routine to have the captain drop her off at the market to sell her bread at least twice a week, where she made quick friends and lunched with other market wives at the local inn.

The captain continued to plan for explorative voyages, charting courses for China, Africa, Europe, Russia, India, and Persia. His hope was to one day sail to the English colonies in the New World. In the meantime, he captained cargo shipments to the East Indies and hosted deep-sea fishing expeditions. It proved quite lucrative, and he soon bought another horse and cart and began rebuilding the west wing.

Not many travelers passed the castle this far north, but the occasional tradesmen would make their way to the castle to sell their services and wares should they be headed in that direction on their travels. Coaches also came by sometimes. They carried what he presumed to be guests to the other sprawling castles in the area, perhaps for parties or balls.

One afternoon, Victor, tending to the flower beds in the court-yard, heard cries for help. He hurried to the gate, and before anyone could stop him, he was on a horse and headed down the hill, where a coach had stopped and a small group of people had gathered. As he approached, he noticed a man lying on the ground, partly obscured by tall grass. He pulled the horse to a stop and dismounted.

"Thank you, thank you," the coach driver said, pulling his arm. "He-he just ran in front of the coach. I couldn't stop the horses in time."

Victor pulled his hood lower. "Help me get him on my horse. I have to get him to the castle, where I can help him."

The coach driver and one of the male passengers helped Victor get the man on the front of the horse. While they held him in place, he mounted. "You can go on your way. I'll take care of him until he's well enough to move."

The coach driver nodded, his relief evident. He took his place in the driver's box while the people climbed inside, and with a snap of the reins, the coach took off.

Victor kicked the horse and got back to the castle fast. He carried the injured man down to the laboratory and laid him on a table. The man's leg was clearly broken; he had cuts and bruises on his face and hands. He unbuttoned the man's shirt and observed the bruising that colored his ribs. He then ripped the pant leg; the break was not severe but needed tending to heal right. Wetting a rag in the basin, Victor carefully washed the dirt and blood away from the man's wounds. He stitched the cuts, wrapped the ribcage, and splinted the leg. After, Victor sat in a nearby chair, thumbing through the captain's medical notebook.

"Victor?" Rose called as she hurried down the stairs and into the lab. "Are you okay, Victor? Where did you go?"

"It's nothing. A man was hit by a passing coach. I brought him here to stabilize him. When he's well enough, we'll take him back to town."

"But… he'll see you, won't he?"

"No. The captain will return him to town before he wakes."

Rose stood behind the chair and put her arms around him. "You're so kind, Victor. Can I get you anything before the captain and I go into town?"

Her every touch stirred his heart. He turned and kissed her. "No, my love. I'm fine."

"Very well. We should be back in a few hours."

Victor nodded and turned his attention back to the notebook.

Chapter 11: Wolves in Sheep's Clothing

Brazil: Marscape Castle

When the captain and Rose returned that afternoon from the market, they found Victor sitting in the kitchen drinking tea. He glanced up and then back at his cup. The captain sat in a chair next to Victor, and Rose busied herself putting away the supplies from the market.

"How's that injured man?"

"He's asleep for now."

"You did a good thing, mate, fixing him up that way," the captain said.

"He certainly did. He's got such a kind heart," Rose chimed in, feeling along the sill until she found where to put the loaf of bread in the sun.

"Aye. What will you do if he wakes then?" the captain asked.

"I want you to help me keep him asleep until we can move him," Victor said. He looked at the captain. "I reviewed the medical notebook. You should use one of the opiate drugs. If he wakes, he's bound to be in pain," Victor said.

"That's a good idea," Rose said, moving along the wall toward the pantry.

"Aye, he would be with that broken leg and ribs," the captain said and glanced at Rose as she pulled the pantry open. "I'll be happy to help."

"We need to keep him pain-free," Victor said. What he meant, though, the captain seemed to understand—we need to keep him alive. To do that, he must stay asleep.

The captain made his way down to the laboratory and opened one of the notebooks he copied from Dr. Roberson's plant book. As he thumbed through the pages, he noticed a long, dark hair stuck to one. He pulled it out and looked closely at it. *Maybe Rose was dusting books*, he thought. That voice in the back of mind tried to get his attention, but the captain shooed it away, thinking he was making mountains out of molehills again. So, instead, he mixed the ingredients and ground them into a fine powder that he mixed with soda water and then heated. He drew the green liquid into a syringe and injected the sleeping man with what he thought would be dose to keep asleep but not kill him.

Later, close to midnight, Victor checked on the injured man. The captain had left a readied syringe on a tray near the table. Victor stared at his hands and hoped he wouldn't break the thing. As gently as he could, and after three attempts, he tied a band around the man's arm and felt for a plump vein. When he picked up the syringe, Victor hesitated; the needle shook in his hand, and he almost dropped it. Taking a deep breath, Victor shook off his uncertainty and steadied his hand. As carefully as he could, he injected the medicine.

The man's eyes fluttered open, but he didn't move or scream. Then seconds later, his eyes rolled back and closed. Victor decided the man must have been too drugged to become fully conscious. After checking the dressings, Victor went back to bed.

The next morning, when the captain went to check on the injured man, he was gone. "Bollocks," he muttered. "We really should have restrained him." The captain hurried upstairs; the man couldn't have gotten far with his injuries.

"He's gone, Victor."

"Who's gone?"

"That injured man," the captain said.

"What time is it?" Victor asked.

"About seven. When did you last give him medication?"

Victor sat on the edge of the bed. "About midnight, I think."

"Was he awake?"

"No. His eyes opened, but they shut after I injected him. I didn't think he was actually awake, but if he was, he would have been too groggy to make sense of his surroundings."

The captain realized he probably under-dosed the man, giving him too little. He said, "Let's see if we can find him."

"Is there anything I can do to help?" Rose offered.

"You could start breakfast," Victor said.

"That I can do," Rose said.

Victor and the captain searched the castle top to bottom and the grounds, but they found no sign of the man.

"Let's split up and cover the road for a few miles in both directions," the captain said. "He can't be too far. We'll meet back here in half an hour."

"All right," Victor agreed.

The captain rode south toward town. Victor rode east toward the next village. When they met back at the castle thirty minutes later, neither had news.

"Did you see anything, Victor?" the captain asked.

"No, not even foot tracks," Victor said. "You?"

"Nothing. It's like he just vanished," the captain said. "Maybe someone picked him up."

"Perhaps."

Back inside, they sat with Rose to eat breakfast.

"Well?" Rose asked.

"He's gone. Either dead in the woods or picked up by some passerby," Victor said.

"There's probably nothing to worry about," Rose said, smiling. "He probably woke up and got scared, so he ran home. Maybe he lives closer than we know."

Victor and the captain exchanged glances.

"Could be the case," the captain said. "But we should be watchful."

"Agreed," said Victor.

Rose put her hands on her hips. "Right, then. He was a frightened and injured peasant from one of the nearby castles. He was running to or from something when that coach hit him. I doubt he'd go running to the authorities, even if he did notice anything. He doesn't even know us."

The captain rubbed his forehead. "That is exactly why he might say something. For all we know, he was simply in a hurry to get somewhere when he was struck. We need to keep a watchful eye."

The next few days were much like the string of days that had come before it, and the captain and Victor began to relax about the injured man. The captain took Rose into town and left her at the market stand while he ran errands. At the docks, he overheard the talkative harbormaster chatting with some local fishermen. He'd picked up enough Portuguese over the months to understand they were talking about an injured man ranting and screaming about monsters in an old castle on the hill.

This was no coincidence, he knew. The captain concluded his business as fast as he could and hurried to pick up Rose from the market, only she wasn't there. Just as panic set it, he remembered she lunched with other wives at the inn before the market closed. He sighed. By the time he arrived, she was already being led to a buggy heading back to the market.

"Rose! Wait!"

She looked around. "I hear the captain," she said to the woman and the driver. "Do you see him, Selina?"

Selena, an elderly, bone-thin woman with a beak-like nose, turned and looked. "Does this Captain of yours were a sea cap?"

"He does! Help me down."

"Sorry, Rose." He turned to Selina. "Ma'am."

"What is it?" she asked.

"We need to go now. That injured man is in police custody, and he definitely saw Victor."

"No…"

"Let's go."

The captain led her back to the cart.

When they arrived back at the castle, José was there in the kitchen with Victor. Victor's pale face and José's frightened but stern eyes told the captain all he needed to know. "You heard?" he asked.

"I'm afraid so," Victor said. "I really thought we'd be safe here. I was actually starting to believe it."

"Well, you're not safe anymore," José said. "My sources tell me that your man—his name is Juan—once treated by the doctor, sang like a bird about what he'd seen when he woke up, about the lab and being on a table in a basement…about a monster injecting him with poison. The authorities knew of the monster in London and knew the authorities there were looking for it. It appears there's some kind of reward for your capture, Victor. Dead or alive."

Victor sank in the chair. "I told you, Captain. Fate is wicked and against us. They only see the monster."

"We'll leave. Set sail tomorrow night. It doesn't matter right now where we go. We can figure it out on the way. Let's not forget anything that can lead them to us," the captain said.

"Another trip?" Rose asked.

"Yes, Rose," Victor said, "Another trip."

"José, can you arrange for a few sailors, enough to run the ship?"

"Of course, I can, if we pay them at least half in advance."

The captain dug in his coat and removed his coin bag. "Here, take this; it should be plenty. You should go in case the authorities turn up sooner."

"I'll make the arrangements and have my men keep a watchful eye. If I hear anything that can help, I'll find a way to warn you," José said.

"Thank you, mate. I owe you big," the captain said.

"Yes, you do," José said and hurried out.

After José had gone, Victor and the captain rushed to pack the cart. They collected the notebooks, letters, equipment, medicines, and plants from the lab; they packed their clothing and essentials. Everything else they'd leave.

"Now, we wait for dark," the captain said. They hunkered down, and waiting for the sun to set, they shared a final meal at the kitchen table. No one spoke; the room was silent save for the clinking of cutlery to plate and cup to saucer.

As the sun set and the captain, Rose, and Victor prepared to depart, José burst through the door.

"Captain! You have to go now! The authorities notified the Portuguese Navy! It's headed this way right now!"

"Are you sure?"

The captain's hand shot up. "Wait. Listen. Can you hear that?"

"What is that?" Rose asked.

"Horses. Lots of them," the captain said, hurrying to the window. The authorities were at the base of the hill, twenty men on horseback. "Well, there goes our easy exit." He turned to José. "Go, out the pantry door, now, while you can! If you can't get off the property, hide in the barn." He turned to Victor. "Hide Rose in the lab. It's the safest place for now. I'll barricade the doors; it's too late for the gate. They'll have that down in minutes."

José left through the pantry just as the officials and their mercenaries arrived at the gate. Seconds later, the thunder of the men ramming the gate shook the silence.

"Rose, hurry. They'll be through it any minute," Victor said and led her down the steep stairs into the empty lab. He placed her in a far corner, against the wall. "Stay here until I come for you."

Rose nodded. "Stay alive."

"I'll do my best, my love," Victor said and bounded back up the stairs.

On the ground floor, the captain barricaded the front doors and the pantry entry. He met up with Victor in the kitchen.

"So, now what, Captain?" Victor asked.

The captain knew the question was rhetorical, but he said, "We fight our way out like true pirates."

"Ah, yes, indeed. Pirates," Victor said. "You do realize the ship will surely use their cannons. We can't escape that. And, if by some miracle we do, we can't avoid the twenty men outside."

"We can and we will. We must,' the captain said.

Outside the front doors, a man's voice shouted, "Send the monster out!"

Victor and the captain looked at each other.

"There's no monster here," the captain shouted. "Just me and my wife."

"Then open the doors immediately," the voice shouted.

"Leave us be in peace! There's no monster here!" the captain shouted.

"I was right, Captain, about fate. They will only ever see the monster, but not even this monster. They only see the monster that went on a murdering rampage in London," Victor said.

The captain grabbed Victor by his shirt and shook him. "We're not dying. Do you hear me? We're escaping." He let go and turned away. "Now, let's find a way out of here and to my ship."

The voice outside yelled, "Send the monster out now or we'll signal the ship to fire!"

"I told you, there's no monster in my house!" the captain yelled. "Go away and leave us in peace!"

"Maybe through the east wing; it's weak walled," Victor said.

The captain turned. "Excellent! I'll get Rose. You go ahead of us. Your strength should pave the way. We'll catch up."

The captain ran to the lab, and Victor hurried to the east corridor.

"This is your last chance. Send out the monster or we will order the ship to fire on the castle," shouted the man outside.

"Not going to happen!" the captain yelled as he turned to rush down the stairs to the lab.

Victor ran across the entry to the east corridor. At the end of the hallway, Victor opened the door and stepped into the ruins of the east wing. He followed the broken walls until he found a spot far enough along and as close to an escape route across the east yard as he could, then he began to pound and kick the wall. It shook, and dust and pieces of rock and debris showered him.

In the lab, the captain found Rose and dragged her up. "We have to go now. We have an escape planned."

Rose stood, and the two started up the steps. Halfway up the winding staircase, the captain heard the familiar explosion of a cannon firing. He threw his arms over Rose's head and pressed her against the wall. The blast was deafening, but it didn't hit this part of the castle. Cannon fire was not an exact science, the captain knew. They still had a chance to get away. With her close behind, they climbed to the door and bolted through the kitchen toward the east wing doors.

"For the last time, I implore you, send the monster out or I will order the ship to fire again," came the loud voice from the other side of the front doors.

As they passed the entry, the captain caught a glimpse through the windows of horses backing away from the castle to the road. He pulled Rose and hurried toward the door. "They're getting ready to destroy this place. Hurry," he said.

In the east corridor, Victor managed to kick some of the loose stones from the wall, and he could see the others ready to give. With all his might, he pushed the weakened wall, "Fall, damn it! Fall!" It gave way, tumbling outward, sending Victor stumbling forward just as the remainder of the roof fell behind him. He sat up, coughing and wiping dust from his eyes. Crawling to stand on the debris, he looked down the hall to see if Rose and the captain were coming.

At the east corridor entrance, the captain yanked the door open and pushed Rose through. He saw Victor standing near the end of the corridor in front of a collapsed wall, waving at them to hurry. Another explosion echoed through the night, and the captain yanked Rose forward, running toward Victor. "Run!"

When the ball hit the corridor, it exploded as though hit by a giant's hammer, knocking the captain and Rose to the ground. Debris rained down on them, and Rose struggled to free herself from the captain's grip.

"No!" Rose screamed. "Victor!"

The captain stood and blinked, his ears ringing. "We…we can grieve later. Live now," he said, yanking her up by one arm. "We'll have to go to the west wing."

All but dragging Rose through the castle, the captain led them to the west wing entry doors. Breathing hard, he said, "I need you to hear me…" He coughed and shook his head. "At the rear of this corridor is a small closet," he said, pointing, "on the left side. That's the only place now that we'll be safe until this over. Once they find…Victor, they'll clear out, and then we can escape."

"Victor," Rose sobbed.

When he heard the cannon fire, he pushed Rose ahead of him. "Run!"

He hurried her down the hall as the next ball hit the wall behind him, exploding like a giant fireworks display.

The captain's hand was torn from hers. Rose spun, searching; he'd only been a few steps behind her, but she couldn't locate him. As the smoke cleared, she saw him pinned under several large chunks of stone, a large, splintered piece of wood piercing his chest like a spear. She knelt beside him and looked in his eyes.

"I'm so, so sorry, Captain. This isn't the way the plan was supposed to end," she said.

The captain, in his delirium, realized she was looking at him, *really looking at him*. She could see. He cringed, panted, unable to move. Blood poured from his nose, ears, and lips. He coughed, and blood sprayed from his mouth in a fine mist. "Rose… W-why?"

"Because it was the only way to get the notes and letters for Victor's experiments. I'm so sorry you won't see the amazing work we'll do with Victor's genius. It's almost sad you can't come with us."

"We?" The captain coughed. "Us?" he gasped.

"Yes, we—us. George and me."

The captain yelled in pain. He watched her open the door to the closet, step inside, and look at him. His eyes fluttered closed. Gasping and wheezing his last breaths, he heard the closet door slam closed behind her.

"See, if you'd paid the penny for your fortune, you could have avoided this fate!" Rose said.

Some hours later, when all was quiet, Rose left the closet and found the cart fully packed with the horse still hitched to it. Not a scratch on either. She fished in the back and found the money, the deed to Frankenstein's castle, and the keys. She climbed up, looked at the still-smoking ruins of the castle, then rode down the hill toward the Port of Brazil.

Epilogue: Blind Fortune Tellers Tell No Tales

London, England: Frankenstein's Castle—One Year Later

Rose and George sat at the kitchen table drinking tea and enjoying the warmth of the woodstove as the snow fell past the window. Life was much the same for Rose in the castle without the captain and Victor, like sitting here at the table drinking tea or working in the lab, but this time she was more alive than ever before, and she didn't have to bump around or play the sad, widowed wife to a monster and pretend she loved it. It was almost endearing, but not quite.

It'd been quite the feat to act blind, to secretly and painstakingly copy each notebook, each letter over the time she'd been with Victor. But then, she was a trained and working stage actress. She supposed it was a good thing that the captain and Victor never went to the theatre or pretty much never paid attention to playbills hanging on the storefronts in London or to the marquee when they passed the Royal Theatre.

More difficult was the longing to be with her true love, and that had been almost unbearable. The rewards, though, had been great and worth all the trouble—the castle, the money, the knowledge. It hadn't been all bad, though. In London and Brazil, she'd been able to see

George at least twice a week. They'd actually been running cons of opportunity in London for nearly five years when she'd met the captain that fateful day by George's arrangement; George just knew a blind woman would be ideally suited to a monster. In Brazil, because of the captain's good nature, she and George even managed to sleep together at a local inn each week. In a way, it'd been quite an exciting adventure.

George was everything, much smarter and more clever than anyone realized or even knew, and now he was an official doctor, too. When he'd told her about the captain and then about Victor, it was just too good, too easy to pass up. George had been at least half right when he said he wanted to share Victor's work with the world, and they would—eventually. Until they fixed all the bugs and could find a way to create a body and mind that would be acceptable to society, they'd agreed to wait. Now it was just her and George…and the man in the laboratory.

When I was in high school, the short story "An Occurrence at Owl Creek" by Ambrose Bierce was a big influence on me. Then I saw the Twilight Zone *episode based on the story, too.*

I am paying tribute to that tale; I hope Bierce's fans understand.

Special thanks to Jeff Ernst for being the beta reader for this tale and providing great feedback and Bonnie Lou for helping keep the story medically accurate.

SAD MAN'S SONG

Michael McCarty

Leonard Cartwright had no idea where he was or where he was going. He was walking down an abandoned hospital hallway. It was dark and dingy, and the walls were crumbling apart.

He tried to remember what happened—but everything was a mist in his mind, like fog creeping across the moors. Thinking felt dense, cold, and hazy. Hopelessness suffocated his attempt to light his mental darkness.

He stumbled to the ground. Reaching up to a chairback, he remembered and re-experienced a crushing, dull chest pain. He fell to his back with his fists clenched over his chest. Leonard gasped for air and mouthed, "Help. Help me, please…"

And his consciousness faded.

* * *

With a fixed gaze, Leo starred at the hospital's ceiling. He couldn't remember how long he had been lying down. His chest exploded in shattering pain.

* * *

He remembered the paramedics loading him in the back of the ambulance, the bumpy ride, the loud siren and flashing red and blue lights. Fragments of conversations about life support. The whooshing sound of the ventilator. Someone had said, "Organ donor." Then sporadic electronic beeps changed to a long, electronic base tone, accompanied by chirping alarms.

* * *

He awoke on his feet, shuffling down the dilapidated corridor. His footing faltered, causing him to greet the floor once more. He cursed and raised to a wobbling stand again. Hesitant, he resumed his staggered exploration. Eventually, he escaped the building, out into a dark and smoky environment.

He looked around. Flames and smoke were everywhere, and buildings, reduced to rubble, had steel and rebar skeletons exposed.

Had World War III happened?

Was it the end of the world?

Was it the apocalypse?

Leonard saw no other people. Not even animals. Just overgrown weeds and crevices and corners filled with windswept dirt and debris.

He sat on the curb. Memories were fleeting. He recalled living in Kansas and that there were no volcanoes in the Midwest.

* * *

"Two hundred."

* * *

Leo wandered the adjunct grounds with caution and stealth. His mind wandered, too, as his grip on reality drifted.

A zombie invasion? Yeah! But no zombies were meandering about or any munchin' away on bodies—no blood smears, not even a hint of decay in the air.

Leo coughed repeatedly. The gray smoke irritated eyes and made it hard to see. He didn't know how long he could continue this toxic journey. Nothing but smoke and fire, fire and smoke.

The smoke thickened. Leo could barely see his precariously outstretched hands.

He smashed his foot into something odd. A piece of trash?

He wiped his face, blinked a few times, and refocused through squinted eyelids. But he couldn't see down. He waved his arms, which dissipated the smoky air just enough.

It was a dead body.

A young soldier, maybe in his mid-twenties, wearing a bio-hazard suit over his combat uniform. Leo realized the smoke could be from anything. The idea worried him.

The airborne irritant reached deep into his throat. He tried to swallow saliva between coughs, but his mouth had become as dry as an ashtray. He hesitated. He had been taught it was a sin to steal from the dead.

Self-preservation prevailed. Leo meticulously removed, then dressed in the suit. He knew if he kept going like that, he'd end up just as dead as this poor fellow. Fortunately, it was a one-size-fits-all suit. Baggy, but he only had to keep the seals tight. The soldier had a small roll of tape on him, so Leo used it to reseal everything.

Now he could breathe without sucking on car exhaust. And as a bonus, he could keep his eyes open. However, smoke still impaired his vision.

Leo felt something bump his ankle as he started to walk. He bent over and shook his leg. He somehow hadn't noticed the flashlight dangling by wire attached to a belted battery pack. He turned it on and was surprised how much it helped. He felt around the suit—found a small bag of drinking water attached to a straw in the mask and promptly emptied it. He was pleasantly surprised that it was grape flavored. They must have gotten that suggestion from NASA.

He had no idea where he should go until instinct hit him. "Go home. Yes, I'm headin' for home," Leo declared.

He was able to see out to about fifty feet with the hand light—it's as bright as a car headlight.

Leo made his way to an auto intersection. He circled it, then stepped to the center, and shouted, "WHAT THE HELL!?"

He spun around a few times. Many of the buildings were reduced to rubble. The traffic light and other posts were contorted, but there were no street signs, no names or addresses on the buildings, nor were there any signs or ads. He reached down and grabbed a crumpled paper drifting along the ground like a tumbleweed. Frantically, he opened it. It was newsprint paper, and it was ghastly blank. He recoiled and flung the aberration away from him.

Panic kicked him in his manly bravado.

He darted aimlessly into exhaustion. He felt his strength leaving him.

* * *

"Three hundred."

* * *

Leo leaned against a tree and played his light beam across his surroundings. He was in a park. The light beam hit a statue—a cast-iron figure of Nikola Tesla sitting on a chair.

"Tesla," he said. "Yes, Tesla!" Leo remembered seeing the statue several times—with his wife.

"Wife," he said, uttering the word. "Yes, I am married to—" The words reminded him of his wedding ring. He poked his gloved finger and could feel the band on the ring finger of his left hand.

"Rachel!" Long, strawberry blonde hair billowing in the wind. Her floral perfume charged his memory and invigorated him. He was the bee drawn to the flower. Her garnet red lips…their nectar-sweet kisses…

He remembered meeting her in college at this nightclub called The Artful Dodger, which was frequented by art students and English majors. He tried to make small talk about art, politics, the politics of art, when she eventually said, "Screw art, let's dance."

There was a four-piece band called Uncle Filthy & The Nasties, and they were playing Berlin's "Take My Breath Away;" he took her by the hand, and they danced the night away and eventually into each other's hearts.

* * *

"Three thirty."

* * *

They lived on Locust Street near the park with the Tesla statue.
"I am almost home," he said. "I'm coming home."
"'til death do us part," he remembered Rachel saying at the altar.
He was struck with the memory of that fatal night and the auto accident. Sometimes a hole in the heart never heals. "Why?" he lamented as despair dispatched pleasure.

* * *

"Again! Three thirty again!"

* * *

His vision rolled forward through Rachel's wake and the heart-ache, coming to the present, to another.

A decade later… Annabelle Thomas.

Annabelle had dark hair, dark eyes, a shapely figure, and a patient heart that loved him deeply.

They dated for a few years as Leo rebuilt his crippled heart. Once he was confident and alive with love, she became Annabelle Cartwright.

Together they remodeled a fixer-upper into a quaint French Chateau-style home. They lived there in endearment for decades. In time, together they moved to assisted living. There, they added several more years of precious memories.

There was a wall, a big, red brick wall that seemed to go on forever. Leo tried to recall the wall. Then he remembered; it was outside of the park, and on the other side of the park was his house.

He looked for a doorway or an opening, but it was hard to see with all the smoke. He decided to climb over the wall; it wasn't much taller than himself. He'd scaled plenty of walls in his lifetime, but it'd been a long time.

He grabbed the top of the ledge and started pulling himself up. He grunted as he ascended to the top of the wall. The other side was even more smoky; he couldn't see anything, so he started climbing down when he slipped and fell, but he didn't land on the ground. Something a lot softer.

"Thank, God," Leo said. "Whatever I landed on broke my fall."

The triumph was short-lived as he realized he was sinking. He was in a tar pit. His was sinking faster, and dread filled his spirit.

He rationalized, "There are no tar pits in Kansas!" Yet, he kept sinking. He squirmed to get free—but the more he moved, the faster he sank.

The tar was almost up to his neck when he heard, "Honey, grab my hand."

He squeezed her hand with all his might!

* * *

"He squeezed my hand!"

* * *

It was his dear Annabelle, and she had held out her hand. They clasped. Leo felt her determination as she tried to pull him out.

Leo continued to sink.

Her grip was tight. She was being dragged in.

Light faded to black as his mask was covered.

Leo released his grip and shouted, "I love you."

* * *

She whispered into his ear, "I love you."

The monitor remained flat.

"Would you please come with me, Miz Cartwright."

The nurse gently escorted Annabelle to the waiting room.

* * *

It was organized chaos, with people running down the hall, coming from every direction and heading into the resuscitation room. Someone rolled in a crash cart. Opened sterile packages littered the gurney and spilled over onto the floor.

From the foot of the gurney, Dr. Wade was reading EKGs and lab results. "Another dose of epinephrine."

A young nurse winced as ribs broke beneath her CPR compressions.

Leo was still without a pulse.

Dr. Wade stepped to the side of the gurney. "Again! Three sixty again!" He raised the defibrillation paddles. "ALL CLEAR!" He scanned the field to confirm all were clear of the gurney, then delivered a mighty dose of electricity.

Leo's torso arched in response to the surge. Then his limbs flopped lifelessly. "PAUSE!" instructed Dr. Wade as he felt for a pulse and glared at the flat-line on the monitor.

The charge nurse stepped to Dr. Wade's side and gently said, "It's been over thirty minutes."

Dr. Wade closed his eyes and repositioned his fingers, probing for a pulse. Nothing… "Time of death… ten-thirty-six p.m.."

* * *

Annabelle heard the room go quiet. Her heart sank, and her head dropped to her chest. And then tears swelled, then flowed.

A few seconds later, Dr. Wade and a nurse exited the room. Annabelle knew what was next.

"I'm sorry, Missus Cartwright, but your husband passed away," Dr, Wade said. "We did everything we could to save him. The coronary artery was blocked and not enough blood was reaching the heart. Our attempts to increase the blood flow were unsuccessful. The arterial blockage was just too extensive to bypass, and his heart was unable to get the oxygen it needed. As a result, his heart stopped beating, and although we did everything we could to revive him, I'm afraid that there was just too much damage to the heart muscle for it to start again. I'm very sorry."

"No," she cried. "No, no, no! My Leo!"

For some time, the doctor and nurse stood silently, solemnly, then offered their heartfelt sympathy to Annabelle.

As Annabelle regained her composure, she forced a smile. "Thank you."

The nurse asked, "Is there anyone I can call for you?"

"No," she said, wiping tears away. "I called his brother. He left Dallas about an hour ago."

"I can see how much you loved him," said Dr. Wade.

She was silent for a moment. "When he squeezed my hand, I

thought he might pull out of it… I loved him… I am grateful I got to hold his hand during his last moments.

"It is a rare… and precious experience," Dr. Wade reflected out loud before turning around and walking slowly back down the hallway.

I've been kicking around the idea for "The Surge" for a long time. I was inspired to write such a story after reading Stephen King's Firestarter *and* The Dead Zone. *For some reason or another, I never penned the story. But when I talked Holly Zaldivar into collaborating with me, then I became excited about the idea again.*

THE SURGE

Michael McCarty & Holly Zaldivar

Life is a roller coaster ride of perception. When things are down, they are really up. And up is really down. I go on the circle of ups and downs and round and round.

August 1999…

I remember the horse's hoof pawing at the shavings in her paddock, her head bouncing to a beat only she could hear. She was a 6-year old Buckskin mare about fourteen hands high. She kept digging at the hay like she was trying to escape from something, but the only thing inside the giant barn were other horses, flies, and fairgoers. The other horses were docile, only a few snorts, neighs, and brays.

Taking them in, I struggled just to breathe because the smell of horse manure and hay permeated the air. But I didn't care. Summer was fading away, like the last licks of cotton candy in a child's hand. I looked at the horse again; this time, she looked back at me, stopped digging for a moment, shook her head, and started digging again.

Outside the barn were trailer hitches, trucks, more hay bales, and in the distance was the Scrambler, one of the fair's rides, which flashed lights and the music of The Red Hot Chili Peppers. Maybe the horse was a country music fan.

And Brooke Allendorf was holding my hand. Me! Jackson Heyward! Never would I have believed she'd be my girlfriend. But we'd been together since we'd both graduated in the early summer, and now we were at the Great Mississippi Valley Fair. She had long, wavy blonde hair and a figure every guy in high school noticed.

"Jackson…" Brooke sneezed yet again. I think she'd been sneezing since we got to the Fair. "I think we've seen everything here. Don't you want to do something else this evening?"

"But I want to talk to more of these farmers. Computers have made such an impact on agri—" Suddenly Brooke's lips were on mine, her tongue tickling its way between my lips until it could play Rub and Shapes with mine. Probably not too sanitary since she'd been sneezing. She might have been coming down with a cold. And I just didn't care.

"We only rode one ride," Brooke stated in a disappointed tone. "There's a lot of cool rides this summer. You didn't like the Ferris wheel?"

"It was going too fast," I said. I realized once the words left my lips that I sounded rather wimpish.

"*Hmmph.*"

"We don't have to stay at this fair. Where'd you want to go, Brooke? I got money for food an' stuff if you're hungry. "

"Oh, I'm hungry, all right, but not for fair food. I got sick on a Walking Taco last summer."

I nodded.

We ran from the barns, laughing, through the dark and the dust, to Brooke's pickup truck out into the parking area. The wind had picked up, and dark clouds, periodically highlighted with searing lightning, filled the sky. I nearly threw her in the truck's driver's seat and then ran to the passenger's door. We took off, bouncing around the cab as she raced away from the Fair down the pitted side road.

She smiled at me. But something didn't sit right. She had that smile like I get when I'm excited about a new idea. Huh.

A few minutes later, Brooke whipped off the road into a cornfield, driving deep into the crop before shutting off her truck. She quickly slid over against me, wrapping her arms around my neck and nearly eating my mouth. Now, this I could get into! It didn't take long before we both had our arms locked around each other.

But then Brooke began to move her arms around, rubbing my back and sides. Then my neck and chest. She moved my arms, too, so I could feel her throat, but when she started moving them down to her chest, I pulled back, fast.

"You think about touching there? Don't do it!" Momma's voice filled my head, echoing over and over and over…

"NO!" I screamed at Brooke. "I'm not going to do that! I'm not ready. I told you and told you. I'm not going to do that!" By now, I was shaking and close to tears.

Brooke just stared at me. She was shaking, too, but she was mad.

"Dammit, Jackson! All summer you've been like this. You know how it makes me feel? Frustrated! I feel like you want more from me when we're kissing, then all of a sudden you just freeze up like some Sno-Cone! I can't keep going on like this! Tonight might be our last chance. You're going off to the University of Iowa soon, and you know you're going to meet another girl who's prettier and smarter than me. I love you! And I thought you loved me! I want us to still be special when you leave!"

"We're still gonna be together! How many times do I need to tell you that? You don't need to worry about when I go to college. You're gonna be my girl. No one else! We don't have to do anything here now to prove that!"

"But I want to! And I know we're ready… "

"No. Maybe you're ready, but I'm not…"

She latched on to me like a starved leech in a puddle full of water. I fumbled for the door handle. When it finally sprung open, the fall from the cab knocked the breath out of me, but it was a good kind of breathless, not how Brooke was trying to suck the very life from my lungs.

She peered down at me, her face shadowed by the cabin light. In silhouette, her hair flying about in the wind, she appeared as a beautiful gargoyle leaning forward to leap from her perch.

"You don't want to play?! FINE! We don't play! Think about it, Jackson!"

She slammed the passenger door, then gripped the steering wheel and dropped the truck into Drive. I had to scramble to get out of the way of the fishtailing bed as she rammed the massive 4-wheeler into a spinout, then flew from the cornfield. You know, sometimes I think they should give folks their driver's licenses based not on ability, but reasonability. Brooke would fail that test every time.

I pulled the few things I had together and made myself presentable before I began the long walk back to town.

I walked passed the tall cornstalks crackling in the night, and it was like something out of that Stephen King book, *Children of the Corn*, minus the scary kids. Storm clouds obscured the moon.

A blue lightning bolt darted across the sky like some speed skater, followed by a bellow crashing of thunder.

"Great," I thought. "I'm going to get soaked."

But I was already drenched in my thoughts anyway, all about Brooke. All my life, I had been homeschooled and taught by mom. She wasn't too bad of a teacher; I learned the same things other kids learned in school, but mom would always have me do homework assignments about the Bible, and particularly about sin. My father was a truck driver, so he was always on the road.

So it was mostly me, mom, and the books. I didn't really interact with other kids that much. And this how it was from Kindergarten until eleventh grade. My Senior Year, my father stepped out on us, and then he wanted me to go to a public school. His reason: I'd never been on a date the whole time, and he didn't want any son of his turning out to be gay or anything like that.

I enrolled at West High School, graduated, and was gearing up to find a college to go to in the fall then I fell in love. It was love at first sight when I met Brooke.

Lightning zigzagged across the sky. This time closer. I looked at the road in front of me. I was perhaps two miles away from home, cornfields on both sides of the road, and the cornstalks were swaying in the strong winds.

The thunder above me was so loud it caused my ears to ring.

I saw a blinding light coming toward me. At first, I thought it must be the headlights from a nearby truck coming at me.

I was wrong.

It was lightning.

I got hit by lightning.

I felt electricity run through my entire body as if I'd bitten into an electrical cord.

I was catapulted into the air, across the ground, and landed in the nearby cornfield.

I struggled to sit up again. I did after a few seconds. I saw my shoes still by the side of the road, and they were smoking. That is the last thing I saw before I blacked out.

Memorial Day 2019…

I woke up screaming. I was in a dark room, lights were flickering, lightning was flashing outside in the murky night, and I was screaming at the top of my lungs because I had awakened from the worst dream of my entire life.

The problem was that it was me in that nightmare for two decades, in a coma, and the world had passed me by.

My eyes were blurry; everything looked like I was watching a 3D movie without the special glasses.

I tried to focus, but because it was very dark in the room, and it had been such a long time since I had opened my eyes, it was hard to do.

I could barely make out that a nurse was standing above me. I couldn't see her that well, but I could see she had lovely red hair.

"Where am I?" I asked. I was still groggy and very weak, and speaking was difficult.

"The Canden House Nursing Home," she said. The nurse kept looking down at me, although she was still really blurry to look at.

"What happened?" I murmured.

"The doctor will be here shortly," she said. There was worry in her voice, but it was still as sweet as a candy apple at a fair. That was the last thing I remembered, going to a fair.

"He'll explain everything," was the last thing I heard before I blacked out again.

Dr. Edgar Scrimm was a tall, balding, middle-aged man, with gray hair; dark, unfriendly brown eyes; and a mustache that drooped over his frowning lips. He kept babbling about my medical conditions Physical damage from getting struck from lightning: Memory issues—recognition and short-term processing—possible nerve damage, hearing and vision problems, dizziness, headaches, limited range of motion. He did say the burns had long healed.

I asked him if I missed the New Year for the new Millennium. He had said, "Yes. That was almost twenty years ago."

"Twenty years. Twenty years," I said in shock. I suddenly like the last two decades zoomed past me like a car at a race track and I missed out on everything. Everything.

Then I asked him when I was going home. He said there was no more home, that both my mom and dad has passed away and their insurance and inheritance was paying for my stay.

I was crushed.

The only relative I could still think of who might still be alive was my Aunt Judy in Naperville.

The doctor explained she had passed away, too.

I felt that my world had come crashing down, like a drunk falling off a barstool onto a wooden floor.

Then the doctor said that he'd explained this to me several times over the last week, and today was the first time that I understood.

I was exhausted and depressed and needed rest.

I had to ask the doctor one last thing: "How long before you kick me out of here?"

He smiled and even quietly chuckled. "You can stay as long as it takes to get back on your feet again. With the inheritance and insurance, the money will flow for a while. Besides, you are the only patient in this room. Don't let that bother you. Getting you better is the most important thing right now."

A few days later, I lay in bed, staring at the TV set, trying to figure out what I was watching. Commercials felt like a mini-series because they seemed endless. The television news talked about celebrities and political leaders, none of them I knew because I'd been in a coma for two decades.

I flipped the channel and stumbled into the middle of an episode of *Mr. Ed*. Horses, talking or otherwise, were the last thing I needed. That was the last place I'd been before all of this happened.

Over the next couple of weeks, they subjected me to all kinds of tests: CAT scans, memory tests, and all sorts of tests with big names reduced to a few letters—tests like MRIs, EMCs, and NCSs. The results were all the same—no nerve damage or memory loss. My concentration and comprehension were improving. The brain and cortical substances were all good, good, good. My body, not so much.

The doctor had Nurse Kennedy oversee my physical therapy and rehabilitation. We started with the parallel bars to re-learn to walk and build more strength for the gait. I had to regain my balance, mobility, and endurance. The first few days on the bars, I felt like I was butter—all my strength melting away.

But after a couple more days, I was walking back and forth. Slow and awkward, but I was back on my feet again.

This regimen was followed by me hitting the sauna and then getting a body massage.

After two months, I no longer needed a wheelchair; I was getting around the nursing home with walker, then a cane, and finally on my own two feet.

I did some research. Built in 1870, The Canden House was one of the few Romanesque buildings left in Davenport. A three-story building with 15,000 square feet, it contained twenty bedrooms, six bathrooms, an attic, a ballroom, and a basement. They have room for twenty residents and patients, but currently only have eleven, counting me.

I awoke in the middle of the night, only to find my dead mother sitting on the edge of my bed.

"Stay away from that girl," she said in a hushed voice.

"What girl?" I asked, confused.

"That whore you took to the fair."

"Brooke…" My mind swirled the name and face around, trying to remember her last name. "Allendorf?"

"She is nothing but trouble."

"Why?"

Before she could answer, she disappeared into the darkness.

When I awoke again the next morning, I had a visitor sitting in a chair, reading a Joe McKinney zombie paperback. When I arose to see who it was, she put down the book.

It was Brooke Allendorf. A lot older since the last time I saw her, her hair no longer long and wavy. It was still blonde, though, but with streaks of gray—put up in a bun. Nevertheless, she still had a great figure. She was wearing glasses now, too.

She hugged me tightly; I hugged her back gently. I was still a little freaked out about my dead mom telling me to stay away from her.

"Brooke?"

"Yes, it is me. I've been so worried about you." She brushed a few loose strands of hair from the side of her face.

I could see she was wearing an enormous wedding ring. "Your married now?" I said, disappointed.

"Yeah. No longer Brooke Allendorf. I'm Missus Brooke Logan now. I've been married to Rodney for almost seventeen years; he's a carpenter. We have a son, Randal, who is going to the University of Iowa to study business, and he's on the wrestling team."

I didn't know what to say. I didn't really expect her to wait for me to come out of the coma and pick up the pieces with me. We only went on a few dates together during our senior year of high school. Her son is almost as old as we were when we were dating.

"I've been stopping by to see you every summer for the last twenty years."

"Why?" was the only thing I could say.

"Because I felt guilty about what happened to you. It was almost as if I pushed you in front of that bolt of lightning."

I still was trying to take everything in. I looked down and pointed to her legs. "What is that your wearing?"

"Leggings."

"They look kinda like leg warmers and nylons."

"Yeah."

"Are they soft?"

"Kinda."

"Can I touch them?"

She scooted closer, and I put my hand on her leg, slightly above the knee. I felt a shock like I'd just touched an electric fence, and as I started moving it closer to her thigh, the shocks intensifying as if I was stuck under that electric fence and couldn't get out, she suddenly stood up. "I gotta go."

Then she left.

After breakfast, I decided to sit out on the steps. It was a nice, warm August morning. I was enjoying the sunshine when I saw Dr. Scrimm standing beside the doorway.

"There you are," the doctor said. He opened the door and stepped out. "Lovely morning and a great view. I heard a battle during the Civil War happened on this hill, but I've never researched it."

I nodded.

"You've been making some great strides based on Nurse Kennedy's reports and your latest physical. I think you're ready to be released."

"Oh." I didn't know what to say. "But I really have nowhere to go."

"I've been thinking about that, young man. We had a full-time maintenance man and custodian named Ernie Blix. He's been working here for almost thirty years. He's semi-retired now. I could use a full-time custodian."

"Are you offering me a job?"

"Yes. It isn't much. But since Ernie moved in with his daughter, he's only working part-time. I want you to work as an assistant custodian with him. He'll show you the ropes. In return, I'll let you live in his old place, a one-bedroom apartment in the basement—room, free daily meals, and a small monthly stipend. How does that sound?"

"Awesome." I wasn't sure if anybody still said awesome anymore.

"Your aunt moved your clothes and some of your belongings here. We had them in storage. We unpacked them and put them in that room. Here is your key to the side door that leads into and out of the basement."

I took the key.

The doctor held out his hand, and I shook it.

My aunt had saved most of my clothes, books, CDs, and a

monkey sock puppet I had named Konga.

For the next few days, Ernie showed me around and what needed to be done. And he even let me in on some of the trade secrets. If there's a scuff on the floor, use the heel of your shoe to get it out; move it back and forth, like you're grinding out a cigarette, it works every time.

The only snag I ran into is when I flipped on some of the light switches; some of the bulbs had burned out, and a few had exploded. Because of this, the semi-retired Ernie gave me the nickname Haywire, a play on my last name and the fact that I was hit by lightning.

We had to clean three floors and the basement. The first two floors were where everybody was at; the third floor was unoccupied. I would clean the first and third floors, Ernie would do the second floor, and we would both tackle the basement. My schedule went like this: Monday, I would sweep the floors; Tuesday, I would mop the floors; Wednesday, I would use the scrubbers on the floor; Thursday, I would sweep again; and Friday was "Trash and Dash Day," which meant we would just collect all the trash in the building and leave after that. It was usually only a half day of work.

There were ten residents and patients. I had five of them, and so would Ernie. My five included Skipper, Mrs. Garrett, Betty, Fred, and Lucy. Skipper had been in the Navy for thirty years and retired for another thirty years, but he still wore his old military uniform at The Canden House. He would stand at his door, watching me mop, and say, "Good work, Petty Officer, keep swabbing that poop deck." Mrs. Garrett would also stand in her door when I cleaned the floors. She always wore a flimsy nightgown, no matter what hour of the day, and would say, "How does my hair look?" And I would say, "Nice." Then she would say, "It is as dry as funeral dust." Betty, Fred, and Lucy were all in critical care, so I had to put on a hospital gown, latex gloves, and a surgical face mask when I cleaned their rooms.

* * *

That night, strong winds were blowing, the lights flickered briefly. Then I heard a tapping on the door.

I looked at the clock. It was eleven o'clock. Much too late for Ernie or Dr. Scrimm to visit me.

The door didn't have a peephole, and I didn't have any windows by the entrance.

I opened the door, and there was Brooke. She was wearing a long jacket. Her hair was blowing in the wind.

She stepped inside. "Did you feel it, too?" she asked. "When you touched my leg, electricity was running through me. It still is." She unbuttoned her jacket and threw it on the floor; she was completely naked.

I slammed the door shut.

"You didn't want me twenty years ago. Maybe you do now," she said, and then she moved closer and bent over me. I could feel her sweet breath on me. She dropped to her knees and unzipped my pants; I felt the soft brush of her lips between my legs.

And I did feel the electricity she was talking about. It was only for an instant. It felt like I was being struck by lightning again. The room was swaying. I was breathing hard. I felt like I was going to melt to the floor like hot butter.

Brooke wiped her mouth and zipped me back up again.

"That was good, baby. Well worth the wait," she said, putting her jacket back on. Then she left, leaving me alone in the darkness once again.

Sometime after three in the morning, I had this dream that someone was using a cordless power drill on my door frame.

I opened the door and saw this big, strong man in his early forties holding a drill in his hand.

"Who are you? And what the hell are you doing?"

"I'm Rodney Logan. You drilled my wife. Now I'm going to drill you. In the head."

He turned on the power tool and bored straight into my head;

blood and gore splattered all over the place.

I woke up screaming.

For the rest of the week, there were no more nightmares of husbands coming after me with power tools. However, when I woke up on Friday night, I found my dead mother sitting on the edge of the bed again.

"I told you to stay away from that whore," she said.

"But mom—"

"She isn't nothing but trouble, trouble."

She started to fade away.

"Stay away, stay away…"

Then she vanished.

It was the weekend, and I had a couple of days off. I decided to check out the fair. It had been twenty years since I was last there, so I went back out of curiosity. Because I didn't have a car, I had to take a bus there. And because the nursing home paid me a "small stipend," I only had enough money to get inside but not to ride any of the rides.

I did have enough money left over to buy some cotton candy, but it got all over my face.

I walked around the fair. Nothing much had changed over the last couple of decades.

Night had fallen, and I was inside the horse stalls. The horses were all acting strange. Anytime I got near their stalls, they backed off, or nayed, or even reared up and kicked at me.

I was leaving when I ran into Brooke—literally knocking us both over into the dirt.

"I'm sorry," I said awkwardly.

We were both on our feet again, dusting ourselves off. I was wearing jeans and a t-shirt; she was wearing a yellow summer dress.

"I'm surprised you're not here with your husband," I said.

"He's still out of town working on a carpentry job."

"Oh."

"I gotta go."

She started to leave.

"Hey," I started to say, and she stopped and turned around. "I don't have much money left to take the bus. Could you give me a ride back to the nursing home."

She thought about it for a moment and said, "I guess."

It was a dark night—no stars or lightning danced in the heavens. Storm clouds were billowing overhead, and it was going to rain any minute. Brooke didn't drive a truck anymore; it was a black SUV.

She headed out onto Locust Street, but instead of going into the city, she drove out toward the city limits, the complete opposite side of town from where the nursing home was.

She parked the vehicle near a cornfield, and it was a major case of déjà vu. I am not sure this was the same spot we were at so many years ago, but tall cornstalks were swaying in the rough winds, and thunder was crashing overhead.

"You shouldn't have run twenty years ago. But things happen. And I felt guilty that you missed out on so much of your life because of that."

I looked at her eyes, and they were sparkling in the dark car.

I put my hand on her knee and started sliding upward, like I did at the nursing home several weeks ago.

"Stop," she said softly. "We shouldn't have done that. That was wrong. A mistake."

But I didn't stop; my hand was making its way to her upper thigh when she suddenly jumped out of the car and ran off. I could tell she was crying.

I ran after her.

"Brooke," I yelled. "I'm sorry—"

That was the last thing I said before the lightning bolt came down from the sky and struck us both. We both went flying like dirty laundry tossed down a chute and crashed down with a loud *thump* before everything went black.

Unlike last time, I didn't wake from the coma two decades later. This time, it was only two months. Dr. Scrimm examined me and found no long- or short-term ill effects, and I only had to do physical therapy for two days before I was back on my feet again.

I thought the Canden House Nursing Home would kick me to the curb, but they said I could have my old room and old job back, and I took them up on their offer.

I was surprised that I hadn't gotten in any trouble or that no one had said anything about me being with a married woman and both of us getting struck down.

I found out that Brooke was in the nursing home, too. On the first floor. But I didn't dare see her yet. I didn't have the nerve.

One day, when I was cleaning Dr. Scrimm's office, he shut the door. It was just the two of us in his room.

"I don't want you visiting Missus Logan. I don't know what you were doing that night…"

"I—"

"…nor do I care," the doctor said. "I had to pull in a lot of favors to keep this under wraps, and I don't like calling in favors."

I nodded.

"Like you, she has been a coma. You can clean her room, of course. If no one is around, you can take your time about it. I am not heartless. But under no condition are you to speak or touch her. Do we have an understanding about that?"

I nodded again.

At midnight, I was standing with a broom, looking at Brooke, in her coma, and wondering if she would ever awake. I felt like someone playing cards at a poker table with a bad hand, busted and heartbroken.

You can't control the weather. Everybody knows that. But in a sense, the weather was controlling me. Every time I tried to step forward, I'd get struck down by lightning. Someday the storm will pass. Some day.

When I was a kid, my family would travel to Mountain Grove, Missouri, to see my grandparents, aunts and uncles, and cousins (that is where my father was born and raised, too). On the trip down there, you'd see all these rocky hills along the side of the road, and I always wondered what lurked in the darkness out there and came up with this story.

NIGHT DEMONS

Michael McCarty

Chase Mason had no idea of where he was. His GPS had stopped working miles ago; he couldn't get a signal for his smartphone, so he couldn't access his map app either. He kept driving on this narrow, twisting, rocky, and hilly highway. Dark clouds kept obscuring the moon, making it hard to see the Missouri road. To make matters even worse, a dense fogged had crept across the road, making his limited visibility even more limited.

He remembered his last conversation, back when the cellphone was working, with his sales manager, Dale. "Chase, you are harder to reach than the last pickle in the jar."

"I know," Chase sighed. "Bad reception out here, ever since I left St. Louis."

"Do you want me to set up the Denver appointment around noon on Tuesday?

Chase paused. "The roads are bad out here. You better make it late afternoon.

"Okay. Give me a call back when you reach Colorado."

"Sure thing."

The road sure was bumpy.

Rough roads.

Rough weather.

Rough lives.

That is why Chase hated driving over this flyover land of the Midwest, flat and boring; the sameness of the landscape was making him sleepy. He was planning on making it to at least Kansas by midnight. And the prospects of making it to Colorado in time to do the sales presentation were becoming dimmer and dimmer with each passing mile.

Also in L.A. was his on-again/off-again girlfriend, Jessica; he'd hope it would be on again soon. It had been a while since they'd slept together.

He supposed he should just be patient, but that's something he had little of these days. When he first started his job, he'd had an ocean of patience, but after all the rude customers and the ignorant bosses and co-workers, the ocean was now just a mere puddle. And the puddle of patience was getting drier every day.

He wished his satellite radio could get a signal out here; it was boring without music on the isolated road. Back in college, he was known as Mix Master Mason, working the weekends at the Scottsdale nightclub The Mad Hatter. These days, he made his living selling mixers and other equipment to bars and restaurants. He made a good living at it, and it paid the bills.

The headlights to his Lexus caught something so unusual that he had to slow down and take a longer look.

Crop circles—circular, swirled-flat cut-outs in the middle of a cornfield. He'd seen photos in tabloid magazines, but never in person.

The luxury automobile went around the rocky bend when the headlights caught something in the road.

Chase wasn't sure what it was because of all the fog, but it looked like it could be a deer in the middle of the road. He slammed on the brakes.

The fog dissipated, and it wasn't a deer or any animal at all.

It was a teenage girl with long, light brown hair blowing in the wind. She was wearing a cornflower blue nightgown, and her feet were bare.

"Jesus," Chase said as he got out of his car. "I almost hit you. What are you doing in the middle of the road?"

"I was sleepwalking."

"Oh." He looked down at his Rolex; it read nine o'clock. Seemed a bit early to have gone to bed and then sleepwalked into the middle of the bi-way. He thought about it for a moment.

"I have to go to the bathroom," she said.

"Where do you live?"

"The next town, Hollow Hills."

Hollow Hills. He tried to recall the name of that town before the GPS went out, but he was sure he'd never heard of it.

"Get in the car; I will drive you home."

"I am not supposed to get in a car with strangers."

"Good advice," Chase said, "Did your parents tell you that one?"

"Yes."

"Did they ever tell you shouldn't stand in the middle of the highway in the middle of the night?"

The teenager shook her head no. "Nope."

"But I am sure they wouldn't approve of it."

"Probably not."

He returned to the car, rummaged around in the glove compartment, and pulled out a business card; he handed it to her. "Chase Mason, West Coast and Midwest National Outside Sales Manager for Kenworth & Parson's Kitchen Equipment."

"Oh."

"Now we're no longer strangers. Get in. It's getting cold out here."

"Charlotte," she said softly.

"What?" Chase asked.

"My name is Charlotte Wheeler."

They both got into the car, and he started driving again.

"Miz Wheeler, how old are you?"

"My mom says I'm 'sixteen going on thirty.' And my grandpappy says 'I'm sixteen going to jail soon.'"

"Glad to meet you, Charlotte Wheeler. Glad I didn't run you over in the middle of the road. So how far is Hollow Hills?"

"Next exit. I live on the corner of Archer Avenue and Hanging Hill Lane."

"Say what?" Chase said. "Hanging what what?"

"Hanging Hill Lane."

"Did they use to hang people there?"

She just shrugged. "Dunno."

The exit had a big, white sign that read:

Welcome to Hollow Hills.

Chase took the exit ramp and turned onto Archer Avenue. He drove along the isolated street. The three things that struck him right away about Hollow Hills: it was a very small town—just a bar, a gas station, and a few houses; that everything was dark; and that he didn't see a single person around.

"Did you have a power outage in town?" he asked.

"Yeah. We live out in the boonies; it will take the local power companies hours to restore it," Charlotte replied.

Archer Avenue came to a dead-end at the intersection of Hanging Tree Lane. There was an old farmhouse with chipped, faded white paint. There was an old red barn that looked like a strong wind could knock it over and a rusted tractor in the middle of the yard.

In every direction from the house were rows and rows of cornfields.

"Is this where you live?"

"Yup."

She just sat in the car and didn't get out.

"Can you walk me to my house. I'm afraid of the dark."

"I'm running late."

"Every ticking minute is an enemy; every minute is working against us."

He sighed. "Yeah. Okay."

They got out of the car and walked down the cracked sidewalk to the front of the house.

She opened the door and yelled, "Mom! Dad!"

No reply.

"Mom! Dad!" she yelled again, even louder.

Still no reply.

"Where are your parents?"

"Dunno. They were here when I went to sleep. Probably drove into Lost Canyon to get some gas for the generator."

"How far is Lost Canyon from here."

"About fifteen minutes away."

"Well, your home. I suppose I should be hitting the road."

"Like I said, I'm afraid of the dark. Do you have a flashlight? I don't want to go into my dark home by myself."

"Yeah, but I don't have a lot of time. I'm headed for Kansas, and I'm late."

"Please."

"I don't know."

"Pretty please."

Chase grinned but didn't respond.

"Pretty please with a cherry on top."

"Okay. But just stay here. I will walk you inside; then after that, I gotta leave."

Chase walked as quickly as he could back to the car. Luckily, there was a bright orange moon shining in the sky so he could see his way back.

He opened the passenger door and pulled out a flashlight, turned it on, and then went back to the house.

She opened the front door and entered. Chase followed her, and she shut the door once they were both inside.

Chase shone his flashlight around the room; it was dark and dusty, with spider webs all over the place. It looked like it hadn't been lived in for years.

"Mom! Dad!" Charlotte yelled again.

Still no reply.

He quickly surveyed the room; not much inside except an old sofa and a fireplace. "Can you shine the light on the curtains." She pointed to the bay window on the side.

He pointed the flashlight that direction.

She pulled the curtains open, and orange light bathed the room. She sat down on the far end of the sofa and patted it with her hand.

"Sit a spell."

"I really can't."

"My mom and dad will be back any moment now."

"Okay. Just for about five minutes, not a minute longer."

"Thanks."

There was an awkward silence between them.

"Do you often sleepwalk?"

"Huh?"

"You said you were sleepwalking."

"Oh yeah," she said. "Sometimes."

"Oh."

More awkward silence.

"I'm sorry."

"Sorry for what?"

"I shouldn't have brought you back to my house."

Chase had a confused look on his face. "Why?"

"Because you are in danger. Big danger."

"From what?"

"The Night Demons."

"Night demons?"

"They are very frightening.

"Yeah," he rolled his eyes. "So how spooky are they?"

"You don't believe me?" she asked. There was an underlying desperation in her voice.

"No. Not really."

"The Night Demons are very frightening creatures. They can scare buzzards off roadkill."

He paused. "Yeah, right."

"The Night Demons are these hairy creatures that suck out the blood and bodily fluids, then drain the morrow out of the bone and leave just an empty husk of a shell. They have sharp teeth in their mouths—so sharp that they slice most of their faces apart. Claws instead of fingernails."

Chase didn't know what to say. "You're crazy. I'm leaving—"

"No, I'm not crazy. I'm alive. I made an arrangement with the Night Demons after they landed in their spaceship and ate everyone in town. They let me live; I bring them food. And you are dinner."

"Spaceship? Ate everyone…" Before he could finish his sentence, there were several loud knocks on the door.

"They're here," she paused. "And they're hungry."

Chase ran to the front window and looked out and saw about a dozen humanoid creatures with dark fur, faces with mouths cut open because of their sharp and big teeth.

Charlotte ran over to the front door and opened it. The Night Demons ran inside.

Chase looked for a quick exit and saw none. He thought of jumping out the window, but there were still a lot of those creatures outside.

Then he remembered the fireplace. Maybe he could climb up the chimney and get out of the house that way. He ran toward the fireplace, but the Night Demons grabbed him and dragged him across the hardwood floor. Their razor-sharp teeth and nail-like claws bit and ripped into his flesh before he could scream.

* * *

Edward Schlack was a farmer driving out on the foggy road. Not much to see in these parts except for the rocky hills. His old, beat-up Ford van was moving slowly because of the limited visibility. His GPS was out, but before it died, he saw that he was headed toward a town called Hollow Hills.

His headlights shone on a teenage girl standing in the middle of the road. He quickly slammed on the brakes and got out of his truck.

A teenage girl with long, light brown hair blowing in the wind. She was wearing a cornflower blue nightgown, and her feet were bare.

"I almost hit you," Edward said, shaken. "Praise the Lord I didn't. What are you doing in the middle of the road?"

"I was sleepwalking," Charlotte said…

Terrie Leigh Relf and I have written a number of stories together over the past few years, including "Moving To Mars – No Forwarding Address," "Hunter's Moon," and "Help Wanted" (all three of those tales are in my book, A Little Help from My Fiends*).*

"Extra Credit" is a little darker story and one of my favorite vampire stories we did together (followed very closely by "Help Wanted").

EXTRA CREDIT

Terrie Leigh Relf & Michael McCarty

Regina Mander hated night school. She yawned, and then yawned again, wishing that she had chosen the Saturday morning class instead. There were just too many distractions at the evening course: Professor Diaz strolling up and down the aisles; Todd Coombes clicking and unclicking his ballpoint pen; Jeffrey Blackwell drawing dirty sketches in his notebook; Ellie Lloyd's cell phone constantly going off.

To make matters worse, Regina's stomach was growling—she'd had a cheeseburger and chili fries for lunch, but that had been hours ago, and the hunger came crawling back inside her tummy with a vengeance.

Then there was the biggest distraction of all: Tasha Prine, with her shiny black hair slicked back with fragrant oil, the Japanese lettering tattooed up and down her arms, her ears filled with stainless steel studs and rings, her pierced nose, her uniform of a black turtle neck, greasy black leather jacket, sleek torn blue jeans, and lizard skin boots.

"It's not a fashion statement," Tasha said when she noticed Regina was looking at her. "I get cold so easily," she said with her lisp of a voice, which made her sound like a little girl trapped in the body of a woman.

The class seemed to bore Tasha, and yet she was there every night. Before class was over, she'd slip out the back and disappear before Regina ever got a chance to see where she was going. She was curious as to what Tasha was up to for some strange reason.

Regina had noticed her the first night of class, how she seemed older, didn't really seem to fit in with the class. She guessed her age to be in her late twenties, maybe even her early thirties. The guys checked her out but rarely approached her. Professor Diaz seemed a bit obsessed with her, the way his eyes would always focus on her with longing—and just a hint of fear, too.

For Regina, it was those obsidian eyes and how she just knew Tasha saw into that place where she hid her darkest fantasies. She shuddered just thinking about the things she wished Tasha would do to her, what she would do, with a bit of shy coaxing, for Tasha.

Todd turned around to ask Regina something, but she didn't want to talk to him. Not since the time he'd given her a ride home and slid his hand up her thigh all the while he was driving. Not since he'd patted her on the ass as she climbed out of his convertible. Todd was so uncouth with how he would bump into her in the hallway—copping a quick feel of her breasts. He had no class. No class at all.

"I told you to leave me alone," she hissed, and Professor Diaz glared at them both.

"It's cool," Todd quickly recoiled. When the professor walked in the other direction, he uttered, "Bitch," under his breath.

Professor Diaz walked up and down the aisles with his hands held behind his back. Occasionally, he would lean over a student's shoulder, watch their hands moving pen across paper. He would nod once in a while, mumble something, and then move on. He rarely looked at what Tasha was writing, though, which underlined Regina's suspicions that there was definitely something going on between these two. She sighed wistfully, realizing that she probably didn't have a chance with Tasha if she were seeing the teacher. If Tasha were indeed the teacher's pet, she wouldn't have a chance at all.

Regina had to admit that she came to class to see Tasha, even though they never spoke more than a few words at each class meeting. Then again, didn't they always exchange some kind of meaningful gaze, even though Regina wasn't sure of the meaning? She often felt Tasha was in her mind; it was just a touch, almost a caress of a thought, as if she were quietly entering a room to check on a sleeping baby, then pausing for a moment to enjoy the exquisite beauty of their innocence.

Regina imagined Tasha wandering the streets of downtown San Diego, stopping at this and that café, stirring her espresso while reading a book or writing. Perhaps she was an insomniac—or maybe she preferred the moon to sunlight. Even though she was beautiful to Regina, there were often dark circles under Tasha's eyes. Her black hair lacked any shine, and her skin seemed too pale, as if she hadn't slept or ate in days. *Maybe the teacher is keeping her up late at nights with extracurricular activities,* she thought.

After class this time, though, Tasha hovered around Professor Diaz, and then they left together. Regina followed them to Café del Noche, that trendy new place where everyone seemed anorexic and anemic and wore slinky black clothes, smoked clove cigarettes, and talked about the latest art exhibit. She knew she didn't quite fit in, but she walked in anyway, waited in line. Sometimes it was good to be around people, even if they appeared to be more hip than you were.

Regina ordered a cherry mocha and found a table in the corner where she could watch them from a safe distance. They sat outside under the stars. Professor Diaz slowly sipped his espresso while Tasha lazily stirred a spoon around in hers, toying with the lemon peel.

Tasha turned around and looked through the window, right into Regina's eyes. She smiled knowingly, reassuringly, and then returned her gaze to Professor Diaz, who seemed so at ease with her outside class. After an hour or so, the two left the café, arm-in-arm, Tasha's laughter reaching above Professor Diaz's low, resonant voice.

Regina tried to imagine them together—Tasha's bedroom must be permeated with attar of roses. The scent of burning incense, sandalwood, no—Nag Champa—would fill the air, along with a hint of something else. Something musky. Something metallic. Something unusual…both sensual and scary at the same time.

Attar of Roses was Tasha's favorite scent. During class, Regina always noticed when Tasha reached into her voluminous bag for the antique glass and silver atomizer covered with tiny pewter roses. She would tilt her head back, close her eyes, and spray the perfume in a trail down her long, lovely neck. The room would blossom with the scent of her long after she was gone. And in the middle of the night, Regina would swear she smelled the scent in her own bedroom, when she was curled alone beneath heavy blankets and comforters.

* * *

The next night at class, they had a substitute teacher; it seemed Professor Diaz was sick or something.

"I'm sure he'll be back next week," the sub said. "My name is Donald Waterman. You can call me Don, if you like."

Regina looked around the room at her fellow students. Tasha was also absent, which was strange, as she'd never missed a class before. *They must be all wrapped up in each other in front of a burning fireplace*, Regina mused, seething with jealousy.

Class ended early that night, and the substitute shrugged off their concerns. "Just follow the syllabus," Don instructed.

At the next class meeting, they had the same sub, Don—bald and fat and wearing a cheap suit. "Still no sign of Professor Diaz," he said. Regina was really curious. Had they run off together? Maybe they were in an accident or something. Maybe Professor Diaz was married and his wife killed both of them for having an affair. Even though there hadn't been anything on the news, it was just too coincidental.

Then Tasha strolled through the door. Regina's relieved smile was not lost on Tasha.

Don-The-Sub let them out early again. As her classmates milled out of the room, Regina took her time reorganizing the books and papers in her backpack. The scent of roses wafted around her. She felt the firm pressure of a hand.

"Regina, want to have a coffee with me?"

"Sure."

"Café del Noche?"

"That sounds awesome." Regina almost kicked herself for saying "awesome," as she was sure Tasha would think of her as a teenager, which she was, technically. It would be another month before she officially entered the "twenty-something" years.

Regina and Tasha walked away from campus, then down the sparsely lit side streets that lead to Café del Noche. Tasha insisted on treating and ordered a cherry mocha for Regina and an espresso for herself—paying with a large bill and telling the barista to keep the change.

While Regina chattered nervously about what had happened in class the last time, and how the band Meat Wagon was going to play on campus next week, Tasha listened patiently, stirring but never drinking her now-cold espresso.

Tentatively, Tasha rested a hand on Regina's. Regina didn't move. She couldn't breathe as she looked directly into Tasha's eyes and offered a weak smile. Tasha grasped her hand, explored each finger, pressing here and there, slowly circling the palm with a long, purple nail. Regina shivered.

"Follow me," Tasha said.

Regina did as they walked outside the café. Between the café and a big brick building, Tasha took Regina's hands in her own again, then placed her lips to Regina's index finger, licking, then sucking it into her mouth. She did the same with the rest of Regina's fingers.

"Let's go to my place," Tasha said, almost breathless, still with the little girl's voice, but it was very sexy, too.

They walked down the street, hand-in-hand, Tasha drawing Regina closer with each step. She ran her finger along the side of Regina's face and gave a suggestive smile.

After a few more blocks, they turned into a loft complex. *How fitting*, Regina thought.

It was dark inside, so dark that Regina couldn't see a thing. After a while, her eyes adjusted, and she watched as Tasha struck a match, then lit a group of candles.

"Would you like something to drink? Some music, perhaps?"

"Water would be nice."

"I'm sorry. I am all out of bottled water. I do have some wine."

"I'm not quite old enough for wine," Regina said, then wished she hadn't, as it made her feel like a little girl.

No I.D.s required here," Tasha said with that provocative smile. "It is a good wine, a Coppola, from the movie director's vineyard."

Tasha returned with a bottle of red wine. "Sorry, all my cups are dirty."

Regina opened it slowly, then tilted the bottle back, drinking a little of the wine before setting it down on the table. She noticed how intently Tasha watched her drink, how her eyes traveled from her hands to her mouth, down her neck, then rested on her shoulders.

Tasha slinked across the room toward Regina, who sighed as the other woman gently stroked her cheek. Then Tasha trailed one of her long, purple nails across her jaw, underneath to her neck, where she rested her fingers, felt the vein throbbing against her fingertips. With her other hand, she slowly ran her fingers down Regina's shoulder to her breast; she circled her nipple with a thumb, then the other, pinching them occasionally, smiling when Regina moaned and pressed against her.

"So soft, so soft," Tasha murmured as she pulled off her own shirt to feel skin against skin. Tasha wound her hand around and around Regina's long red hair before clamping her mouth on Regina's mouth.

Their lips locked with a fierce passion, Tasha slid her tongue into Regina's mouth.

"Oh, Gina," Tasha softly moaned.

"No, it's Regina."

"Oh, Gina," Tasha softly kissed again.

Regina just let it slide because she was caught up in the passion.

After releasing her from the kiss, she laughed delightedly and announced, "I'm going to tie you up."

She led Regina to the futon, skillfully bound her arms over her head, looping the cord through the boards, tying first one ankle, then the other to the slats at the end.

Kneeling before her, Tasha unzipped her jeans and tugged them and her thin, pink silk panties down until she could slip her fingers, then her hand, between swollen folds of skin, between the wispy red curls of her opening.

"Ooh, so wet, my love," she said between long kisses.

Regina spasmed, thrashed around on the bed to the sound of Tasha's resonant chuckle.

"You are going to be fun to play with. I knew I was right about you."

Tasha pressed Regina's thighs further apart, revealing the fullness of her blood-engorged sex.

"So lovely," she crooned, trailing her fingers up along the insides of her thighs, extending her tongue to lap, then suckle the moisture, taking the plump mound into her mouth as Regina tugged against the restraints.

"Oh… That was so good, Tasha," she sighed, then was startled from her erotic reverie by the touch of warmer, more gentle hands.

"Who's that?" She opened her eyes, strained to lift her head from the futon to see.

"Cover her eyes, darling. I don't want to spoil our little surprise."

"Professor Diaz? Is that you?"

"And cover her mouth, too," he added, smiling wickedly at Tasha.

"Javier, darling, doesn't Regina need an extra credit assignment or two?"

"Yes, something like that," he chuckled.

They laughed, and Regina would have joined in if she could, but something told her that she should be frightened, that the fun and games were over, and the real purpose of her being there was fast approaching.

She'd forgotten all about the bliss earlier in the evening as one on each side, they untied her legs, then bent and pressed her knees against her chest. Regina shivered uncontrollably as she felt their chill breath against her skin. Fingers lightly traced the path of the desired vein before their fangs penetrated her flesh. Moans and screams continued through the night.

R.L. Fox was in the middle of a divorce from his second wife. Their house was an animal haven for all sorts of critters—iguana, birds, dogs, and twenty-one cats. Every time I came over to his house, the place was swarming with felines. All of Mr. Fox's kitty problems reminded me of the short story William F. Nolan wrote called, "He Kilt it with a Stick." Being inspired by both the real events and Nolan's story, "Little Creatures" almost wrote itself. This is the last tale in the "When Animals Attack" trilogy.

LITTLE CREATURES

R.L. Fox & Michael McCarty

"I barely made it out alive. They'd torn off what was left of my thumb. I could feel the warm rush of blood flowing down my back, as I leaped through our plate glass front window to escape. I needed a hospital, but I couldn't let these obscenities of nature survive. I just needed to figure out a way to destroy them…" The man speaking to Sgt. Mitchell was in rough shape. He had numerous deep cuts and severe burns covering his arms and upper torso, and his left hand was wrapped with a dirty strip of cloth.

Sgt. Randy Mitchell looked in the rearview mirror as he drove the police car. The half-clothed, handcuffed man in the backseat was shaking badly. "Mister Jolsen, you have the right to remain silent, you don't have to tell me a thing."

"Yeah, yeah, yeah. I need to tell you everything. It's no longer my life at stake, but the whole town's!"

"Okay, then. Calm down," the officer said. "I can't take your statement and drive at the same time."

"Then drive."

The officer glanced in the rearview mirror again and started the car. "Why don't we start from the beginning?"

The man exhaled wearily and began his story…

Matt Jolsen had been waiting for the heatwave to break before he attempted to trim the bushes in front of his picture window. They hadn't been trimmed all summer and were now starting to block his view of the front lawn. He hadn't had time to trim them after starting his new position as manager of the restaurant where he worked since his teenage days because he was now required to be there virtually day and night. The temperature had finally dropped into the low 80s, and Matt had managed to get two days off in a row. The first day he spent just drinking and not much else, much to the consternation of his wife, Katie. The second day, he went into his run-down shed to find the hedge clippers.

Matt entered the dark shed that only had two dusty windows illuminating the gloomy interior from opposite sides. As he poked around looking for the clippers, he heard soft meows coming from the corner. The source of the sound turned out to be a small, black kitten writhing and crying on an old tarp. He left it there, thinking that the mother cat would be back soon. Upon finding the clippers, he went out and began to attack the shrubs.

Katie entered the house and found Matt sweat-soaked and drinking a beer. "Did you see how nice the hedge looks, Honey?" Matt asked.

She wrinkled her nose in distaste and replied tersely, "No, I didn't notice—but I did notice your stench. Go take a shower; we have to be at the Nolans' by eight."

Matt knew how testy Katie could be right after work, so he tried to appeal to the animal lover in her by telling her about the kitten in the shed.

"You just left it there?" she cried, "It must be starving!" She immediately grabbed a flashlight from the pantry and went to the shed to find the kitten.

Matt groaned over his backfired attempt to soothe his wife, then went upstairs to shower.

After showering and getting dressed for the Nolans' party, Matt went downstairs, where his wife was happily playing with two kittens. "Where did you find the second one? I only saw one."

"They were both lying there like they were hugging. Aren't they sweet?" she said happily. Katie looked at her watch and realized she needed to get ready for the party, too. "Matt, while I take my shower, run over to Pet Paradise and pick up some kitten formula."

He briefly thought of telling his wife about his stray mother cat theory, but she interrupted his train of thought by dashing by in her blue bra and blue panties, pecking him on the cheek and reminding him to buy a feeder bottle as well. Watching Katie's panty-clad butt jiggle up the stairs to the bathroom motivated him in other ways, but he went to the pet store instead.

"God, I'm whipped," Matt said to himself as he left.

Matt and Katie had been married for five years. He met her while looking for a hamster for his nephew. Katie was a dog groomer in the store and was offended when he asked her to grab one of the furry rodents and ring him up.

"I don't do that, I'm a certified groomer," she acidly replied.

Matt took one look at the fire behind her blue-green eyes, her long, blonde, curly hair, and the voluptuous figure beneath her smock and was immediately smitten. He noticed a nametag that read: "CATIE–Certified Groomer" above her full left breast.

Katie noticed and misinterpreted his gaze by saying, "My manager can't spell very well. My name is Katie, with a K. I'm sorry. It's been a long day. Let me get someone to ring you up."

Matt always reflected on that day when he went into any pet store. Something about the smell of the animals reminded him of how, by the time they had rounded up a hamster and a cashier, he had invited her to his restaurant, where she had come to eat just before the end of his shift. Afterward, they went back to his small apartment.

"Groomer!" Matt chuckled to himself while driving home. "She thinks she knows about all animals because she was a groomer and watches *Animal Planet* religiously." *Still,* he thought, *she has nursed a lot of baby animals back to health.* As far as he knew, Katie had not lost an animal since the baby rabbit incident.

Four years ago, after Katie and Matt had purchased their house, Katie found a bunny squeaking in pain under one of the front bushes. She decided to try to nurse it back to health. Matt knew it probably wouldn't survive the night since they didn't know what kind of injury it had, but Katie stood her ground. She even called in to work to try to save it. Matt got home that night to find Katie crying her heart out. What alarmed him was the blood covering her face. "What happened, Honey?" Matt asked as he dampened a washcloth and started to wipe her face.

"It went into convulsions," Katie cried, "and I tried to give it m-m-m-mouth to mouth."

Sergeant Mitchell had been a police officer for more than fifteen years and was now becoming impatient with the bloody, half-clothed man. He'd been a beat cop and was now, for the past four years, a homicide detective. He'd seen people do many strange things for even stranger reasons.

"So this is where the story gets a little crazy," Matt said wide-eyed. The sergeant kept the same stony expression on his face.

"Okay, okay, enough with the history lesson." Sgt. Mitchell sighed wearily. "What made you kill your wife?"

Matt looked up at the police officer and said, "I'll tell you everything, but just let me tell you all the details, okay?"

The officer was silent for a moment. "Fine, go on with the story.

You left off at the pet store part."

Matt came back to the house with the kitten formula, litter box, kitty litter, feeder bottle, and some squeaking mouse toys. "But instead of seeing my wife petting two black kittens on her lap, she had four of them. Each one of them was meowing loudly."

"Where did you find the other two kittens?" I asked.

"Two kittens? No, honey," Katie said with a motherly expression. She was wearing one of those long wool nightshirts. "There were four of them. You found four black kittens in the shed."

Matt bent down to pet one of them, and the little bastard clamped down on his thumb. He tried to release the kitten's mouth from his digit, but that caused it to bite harder. He grabbed it by the back of its neck, and the kitten stopped biting. Then he dropped it on the floor.

"What in the Hell are you doing to that poor kitty?" Katie yelled.

Matt stormed off to the kitchen, fuming about the way she had so little regard for his injuries. He went to the bathroom and put a bandage on the cuts. He didn't feel like arguing about how many kittens there were, and all the meowing made it hard for him to think.

He went into the kitchen and got the hors d'oeuvres out of the fridge. He rinsed off his chef's knife to chop some parsley to garnish them for the party.

The meowing grew louder and louder, making it hard to concentrate on making the food.

Matt walked into the bathroom to find some aspirin. There were none in the medicine cabinet, but he did find his wife's prescription migraine medicine, Neurontin. He opened the bottle and took a couple of tablets.

He walked into the living room. "Honey, can you try to keep those kittens quiet? They are giving me a splitting headache."

Matt blinked and rubbed his eyes to make sure they weren't playing tricks on him. He started to feel dizzy and drowsy at the same time. His hands were trembling. He saw Katie lying naked in the middle of the floor, nursing the kittens from her breasts. But she no longer had two lovely breasts. She had six grotesque udders!

Since I couldn't have any babies," Katie said, looking up at her husband, "We're having kittens!"

"The kittens must go NOW!"

He grabbed the knife from the counter and started pulling the little creatures off of her with one hand, stabbing each one as he pulled it free.

Katie kept screaming, "No! No!"

Matt worked faster, pull-stab-throw-pull-stab-throw, until all the kittens were dead.

Suddenly, more black kittens started coming into the room, running in through the door and from under the furniture.

Matt ran back into the bedroom. It felt like his world was crumbling apart. He opened the nightstand, took out his revolver, and ran back into the living room.

The place was swarming with kittens. Instead of a few dozen, there were hundreds.

"Which one do you want me to kill first?" Matt yelled, pointing the gun all around. "Let's play Kitty-Roulette—my version of Russian Roulette. Point to a cat, and I'll blow its fucking head off."

Katie stood up. "You can't kill any of them. They are my children." At that moment, she started pulling off her skin, tugging it off, and throwing the dead flesh onto the floor. But under the skin wasn't blood or bones, but shiny black fur!

When Matt looked up, his wife was no longer human. She was a five-foot black cat. "No!" he shouted and shot one of the kittens.

"Attack!" she cried.

All the kittens started leaping on Matt. He pulled them off and tossed them on the floor. One kitten leaped up from the sofa and onto his bandaged thumb, biting down hard. He was trying to shoot the creature when his wife tried to pull the gun out of his hand, causing it to go off, hitting her instead.

Kittens were leaping onto him. He grabbed one and threw it

across the room—a flying feline. He shot his revolver, again and again, emptying the clip—all the while the kittens kept biting and clawing him.

His hand was covered with blood. He took off his shirt and started to make a bandage when one of the kittens knocked over a lamp. The bulb exploded, causing a small fire. He tried to extinguish the flames with the shirt, but that only caused the shirt to catch fire, burning him in the process. The fire spread to the curtains and the walls, and more kittens attacked him.

Matt knew if he stayed any longer, he would be doomed. He jumped out of the front window, along with hundreds of kittens escaping from the burning house.

He started running down the street as fast as he could. He was several blocks away before he ran to someone's house, pounding on their door in the middle of the night, yelling, "The kittens are taking over!"

"Please try to calm down," Sgt. Mitchell said. "There are no kittens from Hell. It's all in your head. When you started telling this crazy story, I dispatched an officer to investigate. He just reported back. You probably didn't hear him you were so busy rambling on with that story of yours. All the officer found was the charred remains of your house and wife. No kittens, no cats of any kind. We're almost to the police station."

At that moment, the police car hit something—making a dull *thud* as the automobile ran over it.

The officer immediately stopped the vehicle. He took out his flashlight and shone it on the wheel and the bloody remains. "A cat. A little black cat."

Black kittens started jumping down from treetops and rooftops. They crawled out from under parked cars. They came out of sewers, garbage cans, and dumpsters, and out of houses and apartments—the street became a feline flood of black fur, sharp claws, and teeth.

"What the—?" Before Sgt. Mitchell could finish his sentence, thousands of black kittens pounced on him. The police officer didn't even have a chance to pull his gun out of the holster—they ripped him to bloody shreds in seconds.

The cruiser was swarming with black kittens. They clawed at the metal grate, trying to get inside. The felines scratched at the windows and the roof.

Matt started to scream inside the squad car as he realized the little creatures had taken over.

Cindy and I are big fans of B-Horror swamp movies such as Swamp Thing, The Giant Leeches, Gator Bait, Gator Bait 2, Curse of the Swamp Creature, Lizardman: The Terror of the Swamp, Snakehead Swamp, Swamp Zombies, Black Water, The Aligator People, Frankenfish, The Skeleton Key, Frogs, Swamp Shark, Muckman… *The list goes on and on.*

Scream queen Linnea Quigley and I even wrote a book about the same topic called Night of the Scream Queen, *which spawned the sequel,* Return of the Scream Queen. *We are hoping to have* The Scream Queen Saga *(both* Night of the Scream Queen *and* Return of the Scream Queen*) out soon.*

THE FRANKENGATOR SAGA

Michael McCarty & Cindy McCarty

Part One: Frankengator

The swamplands of Florida really don't look like those cheesy horror movies. They are living, breathing entities with several ecological systems, animals, plant life, and one tired camera crew.

"Hey nightcrawlers, this is your buddy, Gary, The Gator Guy," said the tall man dressed in khaki-colored chinos, leather vest with no shirt, and a big safari hat. He talked directly into the camera as the boom microphone swung above him, barely missing his head. "Late each night, I go out into the mosquito-infested wilderness and wrestle real-life alligators for no apparent reason…"

Meanwhile, a few kilometers up the swamp, a short, bald man of science walked into his secret lab. Dr. Terrence F. Dekker was a mad scientist with a big military contract. Because of military cutbacks, his latest experiment had to succeed or he'd be forced into early retirement. The Pentagon was angered about his giant flying leeches attacking some college students on Spring Break.

The doctor walked over to the cage where he kept Frankengator, a thirty-foot long, two-ton, genetically engineered creature created from a freshwater alligator and an Australian saltwater crocodile.

"I have a nice slab of beef for you. Come out, come out, wherever you are."

The doctor opened the door to the cage and noticed the gator was gone—and the big hole in the side wall where the giant amphibian escaped.

"Lord have mercy, Frankengator has escaped…"

Gary, The Gator Guy, was still talking to the camera: "We're here in the Devil's Bayou—one of the most dangerous swamps in Florida—looking for a gator to wrestle to help boost my ratings and put insomniacs to sleep. Wait a minute—that's one unusual looking fellow—"

He walked up closer. "It has a gator head with the snout of a crocodile. The croc's snout is a lot longer than the gator's, which is shorter and rounder. Let's take a closer look."

Frankengator advanced out of the water. The thirty-foot monster hissed like there was a snake pit full of rattlers inside its mouth. The creature kept crawling toward the guy with a microphone, but it didn't like the bright lights.

"Golly," Gary said, "that's one monster of a gator. I'd give you a peck on that odd snout of yours, but you'd probably bite off my head. Instead, I'll grab you by the tail, and we'll wrestle just like the WWF—"

The TV host grabbed the beast by the tail, which only infuriated the monster. Frankengator lifted Gary high into the air and dropped him inside its mouth, swallowing him whole.

Frankengator then sank to the bottom of the swamp with a big smirk on its reptilian face, very happy with the meal. It had never eaten a TV personality before.

When the video of his supper aired on "When Animals Attack VII," Frankengator became a TV personality in its own right.

Part Two: The Gator-Guy

Like Jonah survived getting swallowed by a whale, Gary, The Gator Guy survived being swallowed whole by the thirty-foot, genetically engineered freshwater alligator/saltwater crocodile hybrid, Frankengator.

"No gator can keep me down," Gary said, talking into his camera phone so he'd still be able to broadcast his television program. "I'm in the belly of the beast—literally. I'm inside the alligator's stomach right now. My left arm has a minor laceration that's only bleeding a little bit. Luckily for me, gators don't chew their prey—they swallow it whole."

Gary took out a lighter and lit it. "I'm looking around inside the stomach of the gator. Alligators have two chambers: one grinds up the food, while the other removes nutrients from the food. They have the most acidic digestive system of any animal on the planet; it can digest bones, hooves—and even TV stars."

"I'll cut a hole through the underbelly of the beast to escape. Unfortunately, that will kill the bugger, but that's the law of the jungle— eat or be eaten; get digested by a giant gator or eat a gator burger."

Gary cut into the alligator's stomach lining. The gator started doing a death roll underwater, flipping over and over repeatedly.

Being spun around and around made it hard for Gary to keep cutting, but he continued to slice the alligator's stomach. This caused the gastric acid level to rise, almost drowning the TV star.

"I feel like I'm on the inside of a paddle wheel, but I think I'm making some progress," Gary said, pushing the knife further through the alligator's digestive tract.

Finally, the Bowie knife pierced through the bottom of the underbelly and created a hole big enough for Gary to swim out of the giant gator. Frankengator stopped doing the death roll and floated to the top of the swamp.

The mixture of genetically altered alligator/crocodile blood and reptilian stomach fluids combined with the blood running from the open cut on Gary's arm and caused a spontaneous mutation in his DNA. His skin became green and scaly, and he grew a two-foot tail; his hands and feet became webbed.

Gary swam to the top of the water and peered out with only the top of his head showing. "*I'm usually not that good a swimmer,*" he thought.

When he made it to the shore, the TV host shouted, "Heya, guys, I'm back. Let's Crocodile Rock!"

His producer and camera crew ran off screaming.

"I wonder why they ran off," Gary said. When he walked by the fallen camera, he saw himself in the monitor; he'd become half man, half reptile.

Picking up his microphone, he said, "Wow, now I really am Gary, The Gator Guy!"

All his exertions left him famished. He looked to the path down which his producer and camera crew had fled.

Why not? he thought. *After all, it's the law of the jungle.*

He began crawling after his delicious colleagues.

Part Three: The Return of Frankengator

Dr. Terrence F. Dekker stumbled through the rain-soaked, gator-infested Devil's Bayou. The mad scientist searched frantically for his creation that bad science and a big military contract brought to life. "Where are you hiding, my little thirty-foot, two-ton alligator/crocodile hybrid monster," he shouted into the marshland of mangrove trees covered with moss. "Come to papa."

The only reply was the croaking of tree frogs and the fluttering of egrets flying off scared. The doctor was nervous and wished he could smoke a cigarette, but he wouldn't dare with all the swamp gas and miasma in the air.

When Dr. Dekker reached the mossy lake, he saw his mutant monstrosity floating lifelessly on top of the water with a big hole in its stomach. At first, he was stunned, then he screamed at the top of his lungs, "Oh no-oooooooo-ooooo, someone destroyed my beautiful, genetically engineered creature." The miserable cry echoed throughout the bayou.

It had been two weeks since Frankengator had been found floating belly-up in the swamp. Dr. Dekker had been extremely busy during that time, working to bring the creature back to life.

First, he took a crane out into the marshland and lifted the giant alligator/crocodile hybrid out of the dark waters and brought the monster back to a freezer outside his lab.

The doctor then built a new cell for the monstrous reptilian, with five-inch thick, steel-plated walls; there would be no chance of the creature escaping again.

Dr. Dekker began work on regenerating his creation. He replaced the heart with a pacemaker and installed a microchip into its brain. For the final step, he hooked Frankengator up to several tangled wires that connected to a small nuclear generator.

The doctor pushed the button, and thousands of watts of nuclear energy surged through his creation. Bolts of electrical charges kept shooting from the gargantuan mutant gator.

After about five minutes, he turned off the generator. Nothing happened except a little smoke emitting from the monster's snout.

"I failed," Dr. Dekker cried. "My creation is a failure. The pentagon will force me into early retirement, and I will be the laughing stock of the science community—"

Before he could finish his sentence, Frankengator's glowing red eyes opened, and so did its big mouth. It bit into the scientist's shoulder and then swallowed him whole.

The monster crawled off the slab and made its way to the door, but it was locked. Without a way to get another meal, the colossal critter would, unfortunately, starve to death.

The sounds of the motorcycle could be heard all through Devil's Bayou. Gary, The Gator Guy, pulled the bike that once belonged to his producer up to the secret government genetic research laboratory.

"Hey, Pumpkin," Gary called out to Frankengator. "I'm sorry I had to cut a hole in your stomach to escape."

The cold-blooded monster just snorted.

"I saw what the kooky scientist was doing, but I was waiting for the right moment to strike, just like you gators do," Gary said. He picked up some keys that he found on Dr. Dekker's desk and started trying each one on the lock to the door.

After three attempts, Gary found the right one; he opened the door.

Frankengator crawled through the open doorway and stopped right in front of Gary. It started sniffing. The creature could smell both human and gator odors. The beast became confused and wasn't sure if it could eat him or not—so it kept on walking. Out the lab and into the wilderness.

Gary cried out, "See ya later, alligator." The former TV host started his motorcycle and drove over the horizon as the glowing sun slowly sank.

I was originally going to do this collaboration with Jeffrey Thomas, but he was in the middle of writing his novel Dead Stock, *and I was in the middle of my science-fiction time-travel adventure,* Out Of Time. *Jeffrey came up with the title "Less Than A Ghost"—but we were both too busy to write together.*

I decided to co-write the story with Sherry Decker. Sherry and I did a great kid's book with her Rusty The Robot's Holiday Adventures, *which is no longer in print, but we hope it will be again someday.*

LESS THAN A GHOST

Sherry Decker & Michael McCarty

The cold September rain pounded against Dr. Leonard Nicks's window as if the downpour was searching for a way into the Physics professor's office. The doctor glanced up from his keyboard for a moment, taking note of the thunder storm, and then went back to typing. His workplace was filling with shadows; the only light was the glow of the computer screen. His mind kept wandering to his life's problems that were even more tempestuous than the storm outside.

A vision of his wife's beautiful face appeared before him, a painful reminder of his marital problems. *Melody is in love with someone else,* he thought. *I know it. And the head of Physics, Doctor Soble, is looking for any reason to fire me—and he should! I'm sleeping with Kara, one of my own students! Her boyfriend, Glenn, knows something's up. That's what those boys in the Cafeteria were talking about… somehow he knows she's seeing one of her teachers—*

A knock at his office door startled him. Was it Melody? Dr. Soble? Kara?

Dr. Nicks composed himself before opening the door. For a few seconds, he didn't recognize Josh Turner, one of his students. "Josh!" the professor said, relieved. "I forgot you were still here."

The student transferred his heavy book bag from one shoulder to the other. "I should get going with this crazy weather," he said, "but I wanted to talk first."

"Have a seat. What's on your mind?" Dr. Nicks asked.

Josh set the book bag on the floor and sat in a chair by the professor's desk. "It's about the Light-Stretcher Experiment. I think we should dismantle it. I have this awful feeling that something will go wrong."

"Josh," Dr. Nicks took off his glasses and rubbed his tired eyes. "We've been working on this light-bending experiment for over two years, and it's almost finished. If we dismantle it, not only will it hurt your grade, but it will also ruin the morale of the whole Physics Department. Fear is simply a part of science. It means we are treading uncharted territories, and the unknown is always a little scary. But with science, the unknown must become known."

"Of course," Josh said with a sigh. "But still, I just keep having this premonition that this experiment is a big mistake."

"Josh, Josh, Josh…" Dr. Nicks shook his head wearily. His glasses slipped down his nose, so he pushed them back into place. "We are this close to making a major breakthrough." He held out his thumb and index finger, keeping them just a slight distance apart. "It's only natural you should be nervous. You've been working so hard on this. You're one of the brightest students I've had since I took this job over a decade ago. We must have complete faith in this project."

"I don't know, Dr. Nicks. It's hard to say why I feel this way. It just feels wrong, like some catastrophe will happen if we proceed."

For a moment, the only sound was the heavy rain against the windowpane. "How about this, Josh?" Dr. Nicks said. "Spring break starts tomorrow. We'll be off for a week. Maybe you just need a rest to clear your head. If you feel the same way after you get back, we'll stop the project."

"Really?"

"Really. We'll just put everything on hold for a while. Go out and have some fun. Where did you say you'll be going for Spring Break?"

"Puerto Vallarta, Mexico. My girlfriend's parents have a condo there."

"Sounds great. Now, don't you worry about a thing. Just relax and give that overheated brain of yours a rest! See you in a week."

* * *

Alone in his office, Dr. Nicks watched how his stark, distorted shadow on the office wall changed with each flash of lightning. It reminded him of scenes from the old Frankenstein movies—a stormy night, a scientist pretending to be God, chunks of cadavers all sewn together to create a hideous new life with the help of a mad hunchback.

The professor walked out of his office and down the hall to the huge main laboratory. He circled the room, hitting the switches to the Light-Stretcher, which looked like a small flying saucer equipped with state-of-the-art lasers. The machine hummed awake. It had the ability to divert light through the power of dark matter—a force similar to magnetism, but far more volatile.

Dr. Nicks had wanted to experiment with animals—rats, guinea pigs, or rabbits—but the university had come under pressure from PETA, and so animal testing was off-limits.

There was only one test subject remaining: himself. He programmed the computer to start the Light-Stretcher and set it to run for one hour. The doctor smiled as the doors to the Light-Stretcher unfolded like the webbed fingers of something cold and vile. Once they were completely open, he climbed in.

* * *

The Light-Stretcher slowed and then spun to a halt with a sound somewhat reminiscent of a sigh. The door opened, and Dr. Nicks climbed out. He had expected to be dizzy from the spinning, but he wasn't. He took off his dark goggles and put them on the table just as a fresh resurgence of thunder and lightning signaled the onset of a power outage, plunging the lab into darkness.

The professor happened to be standing in front of a wall mirror when the lightning flashed again.

In his reflection, he saw only the clothes he was wearing.

His flesh was invisible.

Dr. Nicks smiled.

All the years of hard work had paid off—it was like winning the Lottery. Hell, this was better than that—both he and Joshua would get a Pulitzer for this invention. Maybe even the Nobel Prize for science. Not only was his job secure now, but he would certainly be offered Soble's position as well.

He listened. No rain. The storm was over.

Dr. Nicks undressed, folding and hiding his things in the bottom drawer of a cabinet. He left the lab and stepped outside into the night. The only sign of the moon was a faint glow behind a cover of clouds.

He needed some answers to his life's questions, and being invisible, he might be able to find them. With his regular Friday night routine, he never made it home until nine o'clock. It was only seven-thirty.

The professor ran to his house four blocks away and hurried to the back of the building, to the bedroom window. The mini-blinds were lit with a warm amber glow. Three inches up from the window-sill, a crooked blind afforded him a view of the interior. Inside, his wife, Melody, lay naked on the bed, curled on her side. Sitting on a corner of the bed was Soble, who stood and began to put on his trousers. Soble was in his late fifties, with receding gray hair and a pendulous gut.

Soble? What does she see in that potbellied pig?

The clouds parted, and the light of the moon shone forth. Dr. Nicks turned away from the window and looked down at an azalea covered with dead blossoms.

How perfect, he thought. *Now I can accomplish the things I've only dreamed of doing. Now I can make people pay for treating me like an idiot for all these years. For ignoring me, for laughing at my ideas, and ridiculing my efforts. For cheating on me.*

Nicks walked back to the sidewalk in front of his house. Two blocks away, Soble had parked his platinum-hued Mercedes on a shadowy stretch of street. The car was Soble's pride. How he bragged about its price—of course, since he was Head of the Physics Department, he could afford it! Plus, the car was detailed regularly by pricey professionals. "Hand-washed with a chamois, dried with cotton fleece, and polished with Italian wax!" Soble would boast. "I'm willing to shell out the bucks to keep it looking the way it does. Perfection!"

Perfection, indeed, Nicks thought as a delicious shiver traveled the length of his body. *Justice starts now.*

A wrought-iron gate and fence bordered a neighbor's lawn. The gate hung precariously from one hinge, and Dr. Nicks often wondered why his neighbor never repaired it. Nicks grinned as he pulled the metal gate off its hinge and carried it to Soble's car. After only four minutes of enthusiastic frenzy, the Mercedes was unrecognizable. The sunroof was reduced to shards of glass inside the vehicle, as was the windshield and every other window. The hood was gouged deeply in twelve places. Every door was scraped and dented, and the headlights were gone. The trunk looked as if it had been attacked by a sabertooth tiger—one with wrought-iron claws. An elaborate array of scratches crisscrossed the once-lovely platinum paint. A sharp point on the gate punctured the tires nicely—each time with a loud, satisfying *Pow!*

Porch lights flickered on. Neighbors stepped outside to see what was causing such a commotion. Some of them aimed flashlights toward the Mercedes. Dogs barked, and a baby started crying. Dr. Nicks did feel sorry for waking up a baby. He soon heard a siren approaching. As a finishing touch, he lodged the gate in the ruined hole that was once the sunroof.

Nicks hurried back to the college. He had left a side door to the lab unlocked, but now he worried that a security guard might have re-locked it.

Fortunately, the door was still unlocked, and he was able to re-turn to the lab. He put on his clothes and re-activated the Light-Stretch-er. In the back of his mind hovered an uncomfortable thought. There was always a price to pay when one dealt with the Devil—and while the Light-Stretcher was not a demonic presence, it certainly held pow-ers that bordered on the supernatural. The amazing device belonged more to the future or an alternate reality, not the mundane existence of Dr. Leonard Nicks.

But then, maybe his existence had finally—*finally!*—transcended the mundane.

* * *

The professor felt a little disoriented when the doors of the Light-Stretcher re-opened.

His throbbing eyes detected a thin, blood-red outline around every-thing in the lab. His ears rang, and his feet felt too far away from his body. He reeled like a drunk as he crossed to the mirror.

He was visible again—and he looked like crap.

My eyes! They look as if I've been crying or smoking pot all night, he thought. *Pot—what a waste of time and money. It's much more fun wreaking joyous havoc on insufferable enemies!*

Nicks heard a maniacal laugh and realized that he was its source. He slapped one hand over his wide grin and discovered that his re-flection's left pinky was invisible. He looked down at his four-fin-gered hand. *How is this possible? Was Josh's premonition correct? Maybe the*

Light-Stretcher was a mistake after all.

He went to the lab's emergency medical kit, took out gauze and tape, and wrapped his invisible finger with it. He returned to his office and reviewed his notes on the project. Suddenly, Soble shoved open the door and strode into his office.

"You're here!" Soble actually sounded disappointed. "How long have you been here?"

"All day. Why wouldn't I be?" Dr. Nicks asked. "The project is nearly complete."

"What happened to your finger?"

"I cut it on a broken beaker."

"Do you need stitches?"

"No, it's just a little flesh wound."

"My car was vandalized tonight. Totally ruined. I thought you'd be at home, so I went to your place to discuss…ummm…the project's budget. The Mercedes was parked down the street from your house. I just finished talking with the police a few minutes ago."

"Down the street?" Dr. Nicks managed to hide the smile that was bubbling up behind his lips. "Why didn't you just park right in front of my house? Come to think of it, why didn't you call first to make sure I was home?" He paused a moment, and then added, "When you realized I wasn't home, didn't you go straight back to your car? How could a vandal have had time to *totally ruin* your beautiful Mercedes?"

Furrows sprang up on Soble's brow.

Ho-ho! Dr. Nicks thought. *Lie your way out of this one, oh noble Soble!*

"You know," Soble said, "I'll probably be retiring in a year or two, and I'll be recommending you as my replacement. Your future looks bright—you'll have a great job with lots more money. And you already have a beautiful wife! What more could you ask for?"

"What indeed?" Dr. Nicks said. "Oh, and by the way—what were you going to discuss with me regarding the project's budget? I trust we haven't spent too much money…"

"Umm… Too much? No, not at all. In fact, I wanted to tell you that I'm taking money out of some other budgets to increase your funds for the project." The gray-haired, nervous man made a show of looking at his wristwatch. "Hey, look at the time. I really must be getting home. You should go home, too. Be sure to lock up! Good night! See you tomorrow!"

* * *

Later, lying in bed beside his lying, cheating wife, Dr. Nicks rubbed the bandage on his little finger.

Why was the digit still invisible? Hopefully, it'll reappear sooner or later. He also thought about what Soble had said about his forthcoming retirement. Now, if there were only some way to *speed up* that process…

On Monday morning, Dr. Nicks arrived at his office even though the college was closed for spring break. Many college employees, from professors to janitors, would be using the break to get caught up on their work—the place never really closed down. Even during holidays like Thanksgiving, Christmas, and the Fourth of July, there were always employees on campus—security guards, maintenance people, groundskeepers—to keep the machines operating and the buildings secure and clean.

Nicks searched for his favorite pen. He often misplaced it and then found it in the strangest places. It was common, he had read somewhere. Geniuses lost their keys, watches, wallets, and glasses all the time. Albert Einstein was so preoccupied, he once used a $1,500 Rockefeller Foundation check as a bookmark and then lost the book. Such things perpetuated the "absent-minded professor" stereotype, which was not only irritating to Dr. Nicks, but also embarrassing. He finally gave up the search. Hopefully, the pen would eventually show up —probably while he was looking for something else.

The sun was setting when the professor put away his notes for the project. He had gone over them again and again but couldn't find any reason why his little finger remained invisible.

Some minor glitch, he decided. *A power surge, perhaps.*

He kept thinking about Melody and Dr. Soble, and the images in his head sickened him—and yet, they also enflamed his desires. It had been a while since he'd slept with his wife or his student-lover. He wondered what Kara Bloomfield was doing during spring break. Her boyfriend, Glenn Hoffman, had flown off to Florida to visit his family.

Dr. Nicks wanted to see Kara again, but he couldn't afford a mistake at this point in his career. He couldn't take any unnecessary chances. If he were spotted leaving a female student's quarters late at night, it would get him fired.

Then the professor smiled. *But only if I get spotted…and I won't get spotted. Not if I'm invisible. Plus, if I become invisible again, maybe my pinky will become visible when I return to normal.*

Dr. Nicks turned on the Light-Stretcher and stepped inside.

* * *

Dr. Nicks stood naked and invisible outside the window of Kara's living room. She rented the bottom half of a small duplex on the outskirts of the campus. He had decided she would be the first to learn that he could turn invisible. He wasn't worried that she would tell the media before he was ready to unveil his secret to the world. *Would any reporter believe that a busty coed had an invisible boyfriend? Surely not!*

Yes, he would tell her—but first, he had to make sure she was alone in the house. He looked in the window. The curtains had been drawn, but not all the way…

What he saw inside shocked him even more than the scene of his wife's infidelity.

Nineteen-year-old Kara was a petite brunette with a slight overbite and big glasses. Inside, she reclined on the sofa, wearing only a blue terrycloth robe and her "lucky" silver hoop earrings. Soble perched beside her, gently running his fingers through her long brown hair.

Nicks leaned close and pressed his ear against the window, taking care not to fog the glass with his breath.

"After spring break," Soble said, "you will invite Nicks to your place for a secret rendezvous, and I will videotape the whole thing. That ought to get him fired once and for all."

"Won't I get in trouble?"

"Not at all, my dear. You were just a victim of a lecherous professor's advances. Once he gets canned, you'll get your money."

"Why do we have to wait until after spring break?"

"I'm too busy right now. That whole mess with my car has really thrown off my schedule, what with the police and the insurance company and all the paperwork. I'm stuck with a rental car until the insurance pays off."

"Busy?" Kara said, taking off her robe. "I hope you aren't too busy for me…"

Soble chuckled. "Oh, I'm never too busy for *you*, my dear."

* * *

Damn you, Soble! Nicks shivered as he marched angrily down the sidewalk. That horny old goat was the source of all his problems. *If it weren't for Soble, life would be great. I'd be the head of Physics. Melody would still love me. And Kara—*

Dr. Nicks stumbled twice in the hall, hurrying toward the Light-Stretcher in the lab. He was eager to pass through the machine and return to visibility again. He couldn't wear a bandage on his little finger for the rest of his life. At some point, someone would grow suspicious. His physician would want to examine it. Melody would want to see the "cut."

Nicks turned on the Light-Stretcher, and it opened wide, like a palm with webbed fingers. He climbed inside and lowered himself into one of the two seats. That was the next experiment: two people at the same time.

The inner controls were rather simple: four chrome switches labeled IGNITION, PROCEED, PAUSE, and OFF. Nicks flipped the ignition switch, and while he waited for the indicator light to flash, he adjusted his bare rear on the scratchy seat. His star pupil, Josh, had donated an old vinyl seat from his grandfather's '57 Ford.

The ignition was complete. Another light flashed as he flipped PROCEED, and the spinning began. He closed his eyes and counted to one-hundred. That's how long it had taken both times before. When he opened his eyes, the control lights were off, and the hatch was already open.

Nicks raised his right hand.

My pinky is still gone! Maybe it's the timing. Maybe I need to stay invisible longer for the return to make any difference.

As Dr. Nicks began to climb out of the machine, he noticed something else.

One foot! I see only one foot!

His left foot was invisible from mid-calf down. He scrambled out of the Light-Stretcher and ran to the mirror. What he saw in his reflection gave him more horrors.

My left ear is still invisible, too!

He felt dizzy and disoriented—as if he were about to pass out at any moment. As he put his clothes back on, he tried to gather his thoughts, which were racing like mall shoppers on the day after Thanksgiving. He had no idea why parts of his body were still invisible. He resolved not to use the machine again until Josh returned. Maybe together they could figure out what had gone wrong. In the meantime, he had to do something about his invisible body parts.

Leonard grabbed the emergency medical kit, re-wrapped his pinky, and taped gauze over his missing ear. If anyone asked, he would say he'd fallen down while walking in the park and scraped his ear against a tree. As an excuse, it was just odd enough to be believable. He could even joke about it: "It was a dogwood! Its bark was worse than its bite!"

The foot problem was less of a disaster. His socks and slacks would easily conceal those missing parts.

He would sleep on the sofa, just in case the gauze came off in the middle of the night. He didn't want to tell Melody about his invisibility—not yet. But what would he say when she asked why he was sleeping on the couch?

She won't care. She won't even ask.

Then it hit him like a bolt of lightning. *Melody! Soble has been sleeping with her. I'll use his own plan against him—I'll turn invisible, take some photos of the old goat and Melody in action, and send them to the Board of Trustees. The scandal will embarrass him into early retirement.*

There was only one problem with that plan.

When he used the Light-Stretcher, he ran the risk of rendering more body parts permanently invisible.

It could be too risky! What will vanish next? My head? My entire upper torso?

* * *

He finally decided on simply using a hidden camera.

The camera was easy to install and conceal amidst the bedroom's clutter. Most of their house was tidy, but the bedroom was always a major mess. As Dr. Nicks connected the last wire and tested the camera, he wondered how many times he had slipped into bed beside Melody while the sheets were still warm from Soble's lovemaking.

Dr. Nicks had never noticed anything out of place. He had never found any telltale gray hairs or smelled that obnoxious stench of citrus aftershave that coated Soble like stink on a corpse. Was the man smart enough to bathe first? Perhaps Melody coaxed the horrid old satyr into the shower. The thought of sleeping where Soble had made love to his wife made him tremble with rage.

What if they don't meet here?

Finished with his task, Dr. Nicks shuffled to the kitchen to stow the tool kit in the junk drawer. If that little camera trap didn't catch Soble, he'd be forced to enter the Light-Stretcher again. One more spinning trip to set up a camera in Soble's bedroom.

Things are getting too complicated. I need help. Joshua will be back soon, and things will be better then. I can't afford to lose any more body parts.

Nicks took a shower and scrubbed his toes with a nail-brush, as usual. His invisible big toe felt sensitive on the tip, as if a splinter festered there, but no amount of inspection provided a clue as to why the toe was sore, and he couldn't use tweezers to remove a splinter he couldn't see.

It was easier to examine his missing pinky. Later, in his study, he held it under a desk lamp. As he turned his hand in different positions, he detected a faint ghost of a finger several times.

It's partly there. It's coming back! By tomorrow I'll have a whole finger again!

* * *

Friday morning, Dr. Nicks awoke earlier than usual, his right ear stinging and itching. He rubbed it and then rested his hand on the pillow. He blinked in surprise. The bandage on his pinky had fallen off, and the finger was no longer invisible. He sat up, threw back the covers, and hurried to the bathroom. He pulled the bandage from his ear with excitement. His ear had returned, too, and his other body parts were visible again.

"All better?" Melody asked. She leaned against the door jamb in her robe and slippers.

"Yep! All better."

In the afternoon, Melody said she was going shopping and didn't know when she'd be back.

The guilty look in her eyes spoke volumes.

It was time for a new plan.

Dr. Nicks went into his study, took something from his desk, and put it in his blazer pocket. Then he went to the lab and stripped off his clothes. He turned on the Light-Stretcher and climbed inside. After the spinning stopped, he stepped from the machine, invisible. His head pounding and eyes burning, he rummaged through the emergency medical kit and took a couple of aspirins. Within a few minutes, the pain went away.

A thought occurred to him. He looked down at his stomach, and he couldn't see through to the aspirins.

Nicks took the small camera out of his blazer pocket and cupped his hands around it. The camera, concealed inside his hands, was invisible, too.

He left the lab, grinning from ear to ear.

* * *

Joshua shifted back and forth impatiently as he stood beside the baggage carousel. He wished he had a nickel for every time his suitcase was the very last piece of luggage to appear on the carousel.

He had booked an earlier flight and was anxious to get back to the college lab. His fears and doubts continued to plague him. The project was wrong—he knew it. He was certain something dreadful would happen—or perhaps it had already happened.

Dr. Nicks hadn't expected his star pupil to return until Sunday morning, but during the trip to Mexico, Josh's worries about the Light-Stretcher had grown stronger and stronger. He tried to forget his cares and enjoy himself, as the professor had suggested, and for a few days, he did. He and Selena had gone swimming, horseback riding, even scuba-diving. But Thursday night, Josh had a nightmare that Dr. Nicks had turned into a mummy and caught fire inside of the lab. All that remained of the professor after the flames died down was a smoking pile of scorched bones.

Later, as Josh was eating breakfast, the truth hit him. He realized he didn't trust Dr. Nicks.

He left Mexico the very next morning. Selena was disappointed but said she understood and would stay in Puerto Vallarta until Sunday.

Finally, Josh's suitcase showed up. Sure enough, it was the last piece of luggage on the carousel.

* * *

Upon entering the lab, Josh looked at the Light-Stretcher. The machine was off.

A thought occurred to him, and he put his hand on its side. It was very warm, so apparently it had recently been in use.

He went down the hall and knocked on the door of Dr. Nicks's office.

No answer.

"Doctor Nicks!" he shouted, hoping the professor was somewhere in the building. "Doctor Nicks! Doctor Nicks!"

The only response he received was a slight echo from a stairwell.

Joshua's anxieties turned to anger. *Doctor Nicks used that machine!* he thought. *He's probably been using all the time while I was gone!*

* * *

Dr. Nicks figured that Soble and Melody probably met at the Hot-Tub Motel. It was across the street from the mall, so Melody could do some shopping after they finished. She would need to bring home at least a few shopping bags to jibe with her alibi.

It was easy for Dr. Nicks to examine the motel register. Soble had checked into Room 12 under the name Sherlock Einstein. The incredible vanity of the man!

Dr. Nicks went down the hall to Room 12. As luck would have it, the door was open—Soble was standing next to a nearby ice machine, filling a small plastic bucket with cubes.

Dr. Nicks slipped into the room and stationed himself next to the TV.

Soble returned and popped some ice cubes into the drinks Melody had prepared while he was gone. Soble adjusted the heavy drapes, turned down the bedspread. The couple sat down on the bed and began to talk.

And talk.

And talk.

Dr. Nick's heart felt like a lead weight within his chest. When was the last time he'd bothered to have a nice, long chat with Melody?

Finally, they began to kiss, and the kisses soon grew passionate. The clothes came off. Dr. Nicks took several compromising photos.

"What's that clicking sound?" Melody whispered in a low, worried tone.

"I don't know," Soble said. "Maybe the roaches in this place are learning to tapdance!"

Melody laughed—and Dr. Nicks had to hold back a sob. He couldn't remember the last time he'd made Melody laugh.

When I send these shots to the Board of Trustees—anonymously, of course, Dr. Nicks thought. *Sobles won't be kissing Melody; he'll be kissing his career good-bye. The job will be mine!*

When he slipped out of the motel room, he left the door wide open. *Ha, let them wonder how long they've been giving the world a free show!*

He took his time walking back to the laboratory. It was quite amusing, walking around naked and unseen. At one point, he walked past a man sitting on a bench with a styrofoam coffee cup next to him. He thought about taking a whizz in the cup but finally decided against it. He had nothing against this total stranger, so why bother him?

He returned to the lab and was startled to see the Light-Stretcher in action.

Someone was using it.

Of course, only one person would have any idea how to operate it.

Josh.

He looked around and spotted a pile of clothes. Sure enough, there was Josh's favorite blue-and-white shirt.

Finally, the machine stopped spinning. A moment later, it opened up.

It appeared to be empty.

"Josh…?" he whispered.

"Dr. Nicks?" Josh said. "I can't see you!"

"And I can't see you!"

"So the machine really works!" the student said. "I can't believe it! We're both invisible! You sound like you're okay, so I guess I was worried for nothing!"

"So why did you try the machine, if you were so worried?" Dr. Nicks said.

"When I came into the lab, I touched the machine, and it was warm," Josh said. "So it had recently been used. Since there wasn't a dead body inside—visible or invisible—I figured you had used it and lived to walk away from it."

"An excellent deduction," Dr. Nicks said.

"So, where are your clothes?"

"In one of the cabinets." The professor started to climb into the Light-Stretcher. "Since we're both here and invisible, we might as well both give it a spin together to become visible again. That's the next test: to try it out with two people at once."

"Sounds like a plan!" Josh said. "Let's do it!"

Dr. Nicks took his seat and flipped the IGNITION switch. "You can have the honor of activating the PROCEED stage."

"Sure thing." Josh flipped the next switch, and soon the machine was spinning fast.

And faster.

And faster still.

"I'm getting nauseous," Josh said.

"The machine isn't used to having so much weight in it," the professor said, flipping the PAUSE switch. "That ought to fix it."

The Light-Stretcher continued to spin.

"Too much momentum!" Dr. Nicks wailed breathlessly. "It can't slow down!" He flipped the OFF switch, but even that didn't stop the wild gyrations of the machine.

"It's getting hot in here!" Josh cried. The sharp reek of super-heated chemicals filled the small chamber.

"The inner gyroscope must have blown out," the professor said. "I think the Light-Stretcher's starting to slow down. Yes, I'm sure it is."

It took five minutes for the whirling, out-of-control machine to finally grind to a halt. Dr. Nicks found himself surrounded by swirling, light-gray mist. Nothing else was visible.

"Josh?" he said, though he wasn't sure if he had even made a sound. His voice had seemed oddly insubstantial.

He tried to move, but nothing happened. He couldn't feel the seat under him—in fact, he couldn't feel anything at all.

Not even his body.

He stared into the strange eddies of mist that surrounded him. After a few minutes, it dawned on him that he wasn't blinking. He didn't even feel the *need* to blink.

And so he stared and stared—and continues to stare to this day, and until the end of time. For the Light-Stretcher had spun him and Josh for far too long, speeding up their atoms to the point where they could no longer exist in the normal plane of reality. Each was thrown into his own private limbo of eternal mist.

Dr. Nicks was, is, and will always be a solitary entity in a universe of one, out of touch with everyone and everything.

He is not even a ghost, because at least ghosts have locales to haunt.

He is less than a ghost.

C.L. Sherwood was the editor of the ezine Dark Krypt, *which I also wrote for. We talked for years of doing a short story together. The first tale we wrote together was "The Collective," which appears in* Dark Cities: Dark Tales.

We decided to do another collaboration. This time, this story is set on a farm, which isn't too surprising since there are a lot of farms in both Iowa and Texas, where we are both from. The story is also set in the town of Hades, Texas, which is also the setting for "Alone With A Demon," which was also appears in Dark Cities: Dark Tales.

FARMING THE TIMOROUSES

C.L. Sherwood & Michael McCarty

Mitch Strong's new neighbors, the Timorouses—who bought the big farm next door for dirt cheap—had six kids ranging from young pests to teenaged hooligans. Mitch had tried everything to keep those boys off his land. In the first year, the kids destroyed plants, trees, and set fire to a few small structures. Minor stuff mostly. He'd lost some chickens in one fire. In the second year, they'd taken to stealing a chicken or two. But this year, stranger things had happened: a cow, the sheets his wife, Jeanie, liked to hang, and miscellaneous small equipment had gone missing. Mitch knew who was doing the deeds but couldn't prove it. He'd called the police on that occasion (and a few others). He'd met with the same response each time: "We'll check into it."

The Strong farm was small but self-sufficient, and in mid-summer, the vegetable crops were coming along fine. Mitch, a retired Dallas detective, sold to the local Farmer's Market in Hades, the local slaughterhouse, a few of the local mom-and-pop groceries in town, and his friends. Sometimes he sold seasonal crops roadside. The farm made just enough to get by these days, even with the addition of another well and propane tank and the recent switch to solar panels. His dream had been to live off the grid and raise a family away from the hustle and bustle of city and suburban life—and away from criminals, gangs, and bullets, like the gang member with the .45 who almost took him out three years before.

Those nights as a patrol officer had a rhythm to them: beats with a melancholic melody. It had started with domestic abuse calls, followed by an armed robbery or a burglary, some DUIs, and crescendoed with a knife stabbing or a gunshot wound before the dawn. Those were the songs of the night. The sounds of Hades were just crickets and cicadas, and he could deal with those better.

He fingered the small, round dent behind his ear. He should've died that day. Instead, he had headaches, blackouts, a shorter fuse, and a bullet still lodged in his brain.

Mitch had been a good negotiator when he'd been on the force, but those skills failed to sway his crazy neighbors in their straw hats, coveralls, and big rain boots. The Timorous' were secretive, the kids home-schooled, and almost no one ever saw any of them in town. He did his best to ignore his instincts. He just wanted to farm his land in peace. That's when the trouble started with Timorous' kids. Mitch was still making a profit, so he'd tried enlisting the kids' help for a nominal fee but was met with lazy resistance and a scolding from farmer Dan Timorous: "They got other work to do. Leave 'em alone."

"Well, fine then. Just keep your brats—" He paused. "I mean, kids, tell your kids to stay off my farm."

The two men hadn't spoken a word to each other since. His one visit to Dan's farm worried him, however. He saw no livestock, no chickens, and no crops in the fields. Maybe they just liked the land, the open spaces. Maybe they weren't there to farm. It happened that way sometimes to old farms. Sometimes.

After that first year, the economic hits had been hard, like wearing a pair of jeans two sizes too small. Still, he had his farm and a small retirement check. Several of the larger farmers in the area were long gone, their plots up for sale, taken by banks and mortgagers. What he still didn't have were children. He and his wife Jeanie were fast approaching forty, and Jeanie's biological clock ticked twenty-four-seven. She spent a lot of time letting him know that, too.

That second year, he'd gotten the idea to adopt Pit mixes, but those had disappeared one after another. He felt sure the Timorous boys had killed them; sometimes, he thought they might be eating them, too, because he'd found charred bones and skulls tossed over the dividing fence between their properties. He'd gathered some of those bones, bagged and tagged them with their minute tool marks, just in case—not that killing dogs (or even eating them, for that matter) was more than a misdemeanor. Of course, the animal rights activists would have had a field day with this, if they'd known. It might be something to toss in his arsenal if this crap kept up for too much longer.

Finally, this year he'd taken to setting "sound" traps—big bangs and flashing lights—and firing his shotgun. Still, those kids came back like a gang of feral mutts. He was just tired of dealing with the crap and sick of thinking about the Timorous family. Sometimes, these kids made him happy he had none. Of course, his wife would say differently.

Mitch ruffled a few tomato plant leaves. As far as he could tell, the new organic fertilizer his friend at the feed store recommended made the vegetables grow bigger, healthier-looking, and brighter, but it didn't seem to do much for aphids. He bent and checked some leaves. Yep, aphids. But that was good news, really. There are much worse critters that could be chewing on his crops. Fortunately, his wife made a mean organic natural spray with alcohol and dishwashing soap that he could feed into the old red crop sprayer. He'd have to remember to ask her to brew up a batch tonight, assuming she was in the mood.

As Mitch trudged back from the fields on a well-worn path in well-worn boots, he detected an unmistakable odor, one he knew all too well: decomposition. Once encountered, you never forgot it. He followed his nose into the thickets and found his bull dead; it had been shot once in the head. Mitch stared for what must have been a full minute, the blood pulsing in his temples. He knelt. The blood stuck to his fingertips. In this heat, he wasn't surprised by the rate of decomp. Seemed he'd seen the bull early that morning in the field by the house. "Damn kids." A familiar throb teased at his temples. It was time to get to the bottom of all this before something worse happened.

After he walked in the front door, Mitch kicked off his boots. "Jeanie?"

"In the kitchen." Jeanie, who stood a stool in front of the stove, prepared a dinner of steaks and potatoes. She was like a hot chili pepper in every way imaginable. Her exotic looks, big brown eyes, tiny stature, and the put-up-with-nothin' attitude had drawn him in. What drew him in ten years earlier, though, was pushing him away these days. Maybe it was the bullet in his brain killing off reasons why he still loved her. He sat. She put the plate in front of him and took a seat.

"I know that face. What's happened now?"

Mitch tucked his napkin into his lap. "Dan's boys again. This time they killed the bull."

"What? Jesus, Mitch." She cut a bite of steak and chewed. "Did you call the cops?"

Mitch chewed, then glanced at Jeanie. "No. There's nothing to report. I can dig the bullet out, but the Sheriff will likely do nothing the same way he's always done nothing."

She parked her fork. "That's nuts. You should report it. We need that trail of evidence if we're ever going to end this."

Mitch shook his head. "Without an eye witness, we've got nothing."

"How about a camera?" She sipped from a glass of iced tea. "But

Mitch, don't spend too much. We have to make some kind of payment on my doctor bills, or she'll quit giving me the fertility injections."

Mitch held her gaze. "That's a lot of ground to cover for one camera." He ate a few more bites. "Maybe a couple of deer cameras, and I could move them once in a while if nothing happens." He rather liked this idea and smiled. He guessed he still loved her, but she was damn hard to like. "Could you brew me some more of that organic spray? We have aphids on the tomato plants again."

Jeanie nodded and began gathering the dishes.

"I'm headed into town to see about those cameras."

She shot him a hard glance. "Camera, you mean. And don't spend too much." She kicked her stool over to the sink and placed some dishes in the soap-filled sink. "And take the list on the counter, too. I need some things."

He picked up the wrinkled slip of paper. "Yeah, okay." Maybe he didn't love her. Maybe he didn't want kids anymore.

"Oh, and Mitch," she said, "I'm ready tonight. The ovulation stick says so."

"I'm sure it does," Mitch said, putting on his boots.

Out in the drive, Mitch's old Ford sat, and he hoped it would start up when he got in. He gave the hood a pat, "Into town, ol' girl." He got in, turned the key, and the Ford coughed and rattled to life. Mitch smiled.

Town was about ten miles down a winding clay road, and he enjoyed getting out of the house and talking to people—that much of his former life he missed. Three miles along, the dusty road gave way to a two-lane blacktop, where masses of hardwood trees dotted rolling hills. Sometimes, he thought he'd like to just get in his truck one day and drive and never look back. Sometimes.

Big Jim's Feed Store in Hades was a big warehouse on the edge of town and Mitch's first stop. He made his order for feed and vaccines; then he went to the counter to pay. "Good evening, Jim."

"Mitch. So good to see ya," Jim said and held out a hand.

Mitch shook Jim's hand. "Nice to see you, too, Jim."

Jim rang up the list. "It's hard times, Mitch, hard times. I wonder sometimes if this town can take much more."

"Know anything about that family, the Timorous, who bought the old Bradford farm?"

"No, not really. The missus comes into town once or twice a month, but she doesn't stop in here." Jim started bagging the smaller items. "In fact, none of 'em come in here, and that's a big farm. They must get their supplies from the city."

Mitch pulled out his wallet. "Have you seen where the missus goes?" He handed Jim a credit card.

"I think she goes over to Bill's Grocery and Butcher Shop. At least I've seen her carting their big bags when she parks up this way." He tore off the credit card receipt. "Nice seein' ya, Mitch, real nice."

"Same here, Jim."

Mitch stood outside the door and looked down the short row of storefronts. Maybe they really weren't farmers, after all. He got into his truck and drove around back to pick up the feed and supplies before heading over to Bill's. What did they buy? Maybe he could find out.

Bill wasn't around that Mitch could see when he walked into the small gas station-like grocery. He sold quite a bit to this store, but he knew the grocery also sold some supplies. He was curious as to whether Dan's wife bought food or supplies. He strolled over to the meat counter. "Hey, Laney. Is Bill back there?" Mitch asked the pretty, young clerk with long braids and wearing short-shorts.

"No, Mister Strong. He's at an auction. Can I get Tim to help you?"

"Oh, no, no. That's okay. I was wondering, though, if you'd seen Dan's wife this month?"

"About a week back. Why?"

"Oh, nothing really. I had some produce I was going to take by their farm, but I didn't want to bring food they already had." Mitch could feel the sweat prickling his forehead. He really was rusty.

"Well, she didn't buy any food that I'm aware of. I just thought maybe the family went into the city for their food."

"What did she buy, if you don't mind me asking?"

"Just cleaning supplies mostly… I can't really recall exactly."

He found this whole business strange. The family had been in the farmhouse for almost three years, and beside the wife coming in to buy cleaning supplies from time to time, they seemed to avoid venturing into town. "Do you think Bill'll be in later today?" Mitch asked.

"Don't think so," she said and popped her gum. "Should be back tomorrow, though."

"Just tell him I stopped in."

"Sure thing, Mister Strong."

Mitch gave the pretty, yet somehow trashy clerk a nod and headed out to visit Sheriff Mark Mann, a man Mitch didn't much care for. He thought of that office as a crew of the laziest police officers in the state.

In the middle of the municipal complex, nestled between the Hades Municipal Court and Hades's City Department, the Sheriff's Department consisted of twenty employees, twelve of whom were officers. Mitch found Sheriff Mark Mann hunched over a laptop on a beat-up desk chair. "Mark, got a minute?"

Mark turned off his computer and tipped forward. "Sure, sure. Have a seat. I've been a little backed up since Deputy Quinn Navarro took a leave of absence because his father is dying. What can I do for you today, Mitch? "

Mitch sat. "Someone killed my bull this morning."

"Well, now, Mitch, you know you have to file a report at the desk for that."

"I've filed reports for three years, and nothing has ever been done." Mitch leaned forward. "I want something done."

"Crimes like this are difficult to solve. You know that."

"I know who's doing this, Mark. It's those Timorous kids, probably the older ones. Three of the farms near me are vacant and for sale. Dan lives right behind me. Now you tell me it's not them."

"It may well be, Mitch, but I need proof."

"Have you ever sent anyone out to investigate or to talk to Dan?"

"Well, yes. But Dan denies his kids have ever been on your property." Mark picked up a pen and started tapping it on the desk. "It's a tricky situation. I got nothing. Look, just file the report. We need that paper trail in case anything does come of all this."

Mitch leaned back and sighed. "What if I could get some evidence?"

"Well, that would be the first step now, wouldn't it."

"I have an idea to use hidden cameras. Will that work for you?"

"Well, it's legal anyway."

"Okay, Mark, thanks." *For not a damn thing*, he thought. He shook the sheriff's hand and worked his way back to the desk, where he filled out a one-page form report.

As the door slammed behind him on his way out, his fuse ignited, and by the time he reached the truck, he was fuming. He got in and drove to Hunter's Merch Store a few miles away. He bought four deer cameras and some odds and ends to mount them.

After leaving Hunter's, Mitch went to see his physician, Dr. Browne. He needed to visit him in person to get his pain medication, partly because he had to for the prescription and partly because the doctor wanted a progress report on Jeanie and the whole pregnancy nightmare.

"Here's my mug, so where's my drugs," he joked when the doctor walked in.

By the time Mitch arrived home, the sun was on the horizon. He'd have to be quick to get the cameras in place before it was fully dark. He transferred the equipment onto an RTV and headed out to the southern fence line where he'd found the bones. Concealed behind the tree line, Mitch climbed a deer stand ladder and looked out over the Timorous land: barren except for charred barrels and pits. He fixed the first camera to the peephole, checked the view, and climbed down.

The next stop was his east field and a long thicket that ran the interior fence line. He donned heavy gloves and set up this camera, looking out and up toward the field. Next, he drove to the western fence, where a grove of Pecan trees obscured the fence. He mounted the third camera in the center of the field facing his house. Last, he mounted a camera on a branch in an old oak tree in his front yard facing the house.

By the time he came indoors, he was exhausted, and his head throbbed. Maybe he'd catch the sons of bitches this time. He'd never thought he'd hear himself thinking about kids in such a negative light, but these, he was almost sure, were not human children, but the spawn of Satan himself. "Jeanie?"

"Up here."

Mitch kicked off his boots and climbed the steps. Jeanie lay on the bed, her ovulation kit on the nightstand. "I need a shower," he said.

"Just hurry. We only have a window of a few hours." She pulled the covers over her.

Mitch stared at her for a long moment, nodded, and headed for the shower.

When he finished his shower, Jeanie's butt was propped on pillows, and she was reading another ovulation stick.

Mitch remembered when they were dating: she wore lingerie, they had marathon lovemaking nights, and occasionally, a pair of his handcuffs would end up dangling on her brass bed.

Now, handcuffs were out and frumpy housecoats, and quickies to get her pregnant were in.

He popped the jagged, little blue pill into his mouth and followed that with a glass of water. He sighed, and his head began to throb harder.

The next morning, Mitch was up early. He wanted to check the deer cams before he started his chores. He poured a cup of coffee, and when he opened the front door, the cup fell from his fingers. Two chickens lay on the porch, their heads a few feet away. Blood spattered the railings, steps, door, and window. Between them sat one of the deer cams. Mitch knelt and picked it up. He took it and the cup back inside, where he refilled the coffee cup before sitting at the kitchen table. His hands shook, but it wasn't fear. Hell no. It was anger.

He pulled the camera out of the box and viewed it. The chicken carnage played back, but he only saw fingertips, a palm, and several pairs of boots, but it might be enough. He took the camera to his office and plugged it into his computer. After the pictures finished uploading, he put the camera in his front pocket.

Before he could do anything else, he had to clean up the mess.

Later, at the station, Mitch sat across from the Sheriff, and they watched the film together.

Sheriff Mann took off his hat and scratched his bald head. "You're still not giving much here," he said.

"It does constitute proof that a person, or persons, is coming on my farm and destroying my property and killing my livestock," Mitch rebutted.

"Yes, it does." The sheriff took a sip of coffee. "But Mitch, it doesn't show who. It could be anyone."

"With the past reports I filed against the Timorouses, this should make them prime suspects."

"It just shows two neighbors are feuding with each other, not much more. As a former law officer, you should know that."

"Damn it, Mark. Are you going to let them get away with murder? Chickens aren't cheap."

"I didn't say that either." The sheriff put down his cup of coffee. "You're familiar with scared straight, right?"

"Yeah, yeah, I know. Taking juvenile delinquents to jail and letting them talk with inmates to deter them from doing stupid shit and ending up in jail, scaring them away from future crimes. What about it?"

"I want to show this film to the Timorouses. Tell them your property is now under constant surveillance. It might scare them away from returning to your farm to do any more damage."

Mitch thought about it for a couple of moments. "I've done similar stuff when I worked in Dallas with gangs. It does work. Okay. Under one condition."

"What's that?"

"After you finish talking with the Timorouses, you come over to my house immediately and tell me everything."

"I can do that. I'll head over to the Tumouruses right now. I'll let you know what happens afterward." The Sheriff put his hat back on, stood up, and walked out the door.

Mitch spent the afternoon working in the organic tomatoes garden: picking the ripe tomatoes, pulling the weeds, fertilizing the plants that needed it. He reminisced about his old neighbors, the Bradfords, who had the place before the Timorouses. They would plant corn every year, and the crops were the color of sunshine in the summer and the color of dusk during the fall. Now, the only color was a barren landscape.

The next thing he knew, the sun was slowly sinking over the horizon.

"What the hell," he said to himself. "Where the hell is the sheriff? Did he forget about me? Absent-minded old coot." He walked out of the garden and looked across to the neighbor's farm, and sure enough, the squad car was still parked in the gravel driveway. "What's he doing? A marathon of scared straight?"

Something in his gut didn't feel right. He walked back inside his house and grabbed his .22, shoving it in his back pocket, and marched over to the Timorouses.

Mitch wasn't planning on knocking on the door. He was planning on barging in. People in these parts rarely locked their front doors. As he approached the door, he slowed. It stood wide open. He pulled the gun, instincts taking over, and crept into the house. Blood everywhere, like someone put a bucket of the stuff on a turntable. Despite a career filled with bloody crime scenes, what he witnessed turned his stomach.

The sheriff lay dead on the floor and all the Timorous kids were down on all fours, eating his flesh and internal organs. They sounded like hungry wolves devouring a wild boar. For half a ridiculous moment, Mitch thought of Jeanie and her ovulation stick. His head really throbbed. In a far corner were the remains, at least that's what his fevered brain thought, of people and animals. The place was rank with the scent of rotting flesh, and the coppery flavor of blood sat heavily on his tongue.

"I have growing children," Dan said. He sat lounging in his recliner, watching the evening news, picking his teeth with a sliver of a bone. "They need to eat."

"This is—just... You and your kids are sick, deranged," Mitch said. "I won't let you—"

The strike landed on his arm. Mitch's mind raced, and his eyes widened as he watched Dan's razor-sharp, bloodstained teeth sink into the flesh of his arm. Colors danced in front of his eyes, followed by blinding pain. The .22 was still in his other hand, raised to Dan's face. Mitch fired. Dan's head jerked sideways, and he fell back in the chair, Mitch's flesh between his teeth, his blood leaking from those lips.

Mitch turned, gun still raised. The six Timorous kids growled like a pack of angry dogs. They leaped at Mitch, and he dodged the first two, shooting one of the youngest in the head—the boy sliding to stop by his father's feet. The second boy landed a bite on Mitch's leg, and Mitch yowled in pain. He shot the kid in the top of the head just as the older boys slammed Mitch to the floor, clawing at him like a herd of hungry jackals, tearing and eating his flesh.

Mitch struggled to focus and bring the gun up. He shot until the gun clicked, over and over. He realized all the rabid dogs were dead and that his own blood was spreading out around him on the floor. Despite all the blood loss of the Timorous' dogs, or whatever they were, none of their bites had hit anything vital. The world spun out of focus, but Mitch did not go "quietly into that good night."

A few hours later, Mitch awoke. The room stank of dog and blood and old guts. With all his strength, he managed to pull himself up again. His wounds seeped, and he felt weak, like an old car battery before it finally dies. Still, there was work to do, and his feverish mind had a plan. First, he'd heft the bodies into a wagon and haul them out to the north field, where he'd spend the rest of the day bury-ing them deep near a boulder and some shrub. Then he would return to the Timorous' house, open the gas valve, turn on the gas stove, and blow out the pilot light. He'd then light a candle near the stove and leave. He'd be long gone before what little "law enforcement" remained in this hick town or the volunteer fire department showed up.

"Maybe the bullet in my brain killed the part that loved Jeanine," Mitch mumbled.

"Or maybe you're just a fool," Dan said, standing behind him. "Did you think bullets would kill us?"

At that moment, all his children were standing next to him, and they leaped on Mitch like a pack of hungry junkyard dogs attacking a rat for food.

Mitch didn't even have time to scream. His last thoughts were of Jeanie. "She'll never get pregnant now."

FRANKENSTEIN'S MISTRESS AFTERWORD

THE STRANGE CASE OF MICHAEL McCARTY

Cristopher DeRose

In a former life, Michael McCarty must have been a mad scientist. Hell, he could be one in his current life.

Lest you misunderstand, this is meant with respect. I mean, I don't know anyone other than Mike who would open a book stating he'd wanted to write a sequel to the landmark *Frankenstein* since he was in college, let alone do it. That says something about a writer, and in the case of Michael McCarty, it exhibits the confidence of a man who knows what he's doing and loves every second. He is a devotee of the genres he visits and enjoys creating these things as much as his readers love reading them.

While madness can be a motivating force for misguided endeavors, like our good Frankenstein has demonstrated, a certain madness entertains and maybe even enlightens. And in this respect, our Mr. McCarty is quite mad, indeed.

In this collection, Mike gave a tip of the hat to his influences and his collaborators and gave them their specific due. It's a unique experience, to say the least. Not everybody does such things. Here, the author doffs his hat politely and wanders through fields familiar to the likes of

Ambrose Bierce, Stephen King, and Mary Shelley, and he does it with a wide smile.

Every good mad scientist has a castle. I just call it Mike's Mind. He still sees the value of the child's game of What If, and we are the better for it.

And to the author, I must say thanks for showing us around a few rooms in your castle.

Exit through the gift shop.

Los Angeles, 2020

ABOUT THE AUTHORS

MICHAEL McCARTY has been a professional writer since 1983, and the author of over forty-five books, including *Dark Cities: Dark Tales; A Little Help from My Fiends; Liquid Diet & Midnight Snack; Dark Duets; Apocalypse America!* (co-written with Mark McLaughlin); *Dracula Transformed and Other Bloodthirsty Tales* (also with Mark McLaughlin); *Lost Girl of the Lake* (with Joe McKinney); and the vampire series, *Bloodless: Bloodless, Bloodlust,* and *Bloodline* (co-written with Jody LaGreca). He is a five-time Bram Stoker Finalist, and in 2008, he won the David R. Collins' Literary Achievement Award from the Midwest Writing Center.

His nonfiction books include: *Ghosts of the Quad Cities* (co-written with Mark McLaughlin) and *Modern Mythmakers: 35 Interviews with Horror and Science Fiction Writers and Filmmakers,* which features interviews with Ray Bradbury, Dean Koontz, John Carpenter, Richard Matheson, Elvira, Linnea Quigley, John Saul, Joe McKinney, and many more.

Michael McCarty lives in Rock Island, Illinois, with his wife, Cindy, and pet rabbit, Yeti.

Michael McCarty is on Twitter as michaelmccarty6.
His blog site is at: http://monstermikeyaauthor.wordpress.com
Facebook! Like him on his official page: http://www.facebook.com/michaelmccarty.horror.

C. DEAN ANDERSSON writes horror and fantasy with an edge. Author Graham Masterton describes Dean's writing as "fearsome and up-front." Writer John Steakley claims Dean's books are "like Stephen King, only scary." *Publisher's Weekly* deemed Dean's Sword and Sorcery work to be "The Heavy Metal of Fantasy Adventure." His epic Vampire novel, *I Am Dracula,* was featured in director Amy Hesketh's Vampire film, *Olalla,* and received a Count Dracula Fan Club recommendation. The SF magazine *Locus* praised Dean's novel *Fiend.* The Cemetery Dance short story, "The Death Wagon Rolls on By," earned a Horror Writers Association Bram Stoker Finalist award. Dean's books are available from Crossroad Press in new digital editions, Amazon, and all the usual sources in all formats.

CRISTOPHER DeROSE is a father, writer, photographer, and musician, Cristopher has had over 100 works published in the likes of *Filmax* and *Cemetery Dance*, and was a Staff Writer for the (then-spelled) *Sci-Fi Channel* for several years. He worked as Editor for *Dark Matter Magazine: A Chronicle of the Speculative Mind* for its three-year run. His books range from the non-fiction, the *Scribes of Speculative Fiction* series, as well as fiction, including: *To Cast a Violent Shadow, Black Moon, Immortals, The Quicksilver Waltz,* and *The Quality of Mercy.* He lives in Los Angeles.

SHERRY DECKER lives in Washington state and has written a collection of short fiction titled *Hook House and Other Horrors,* a futuristic earth novel titled *Hypershot,* and a literary horror novel called *A Summer with the Dead.* Her short fiction has appeared in publications such as *Cemetery Dance, Black Gate, Dark Wisdom,* and *Alfred Hitchcock's Mystery Magazine.* Her story "Hicklebickle Rock" won first place in the North Texas Professional Writers Association, and she has been a finalist in various contests, including Writers of the Future and the Pacific Northwest Writers Association genre contest. She also edited and published, *Indigenous Fiction: wondrously weird and offbeat* from 1997 to 2001.

R. L. FOX As a military veteran, R.L. Fox has been involved in dark places like Panama, Saudi Arabia, Iraq, and South Korea (he won't even speak of the mission he was involved in to the North). He has shown himself to the world to be unbreakable. His fiction and poetry on the other hand (when he surfaces long enough to write and submit it) is groundbreaking and has appeared in such magazines as *Frightmares, The Reaper, Goddess Of The Bay, Mad Scientist,* and *Dark Krypt.* He appeared in the short story collections *Dark Duets* by Michael McCarty, *Little Creatures* by Michael McCarty, and *A Little Help from My Fiends* by Michael McCarty. He has appeared in *Attack of the Two-Headed Poetry Monster* by Michael McCarty & Mark McLaughlin, *Revenge of the Two-Headed Poetry Monster* by Michael McCarty & Mark McLaughlin, *Bride of the Two-Headed Poetry Monster* by Michael McCarty & Mark McLaugh-lin, and *Fear & Desire* by S.A. Gambino & Michael McCarty.

CINDY McCARTY is wife to horror writer Michael McCarty, rabbit mom to Yeti the Bunny, and a singer in the band Beach Party Zombies. Her work has appeared in such books as *Small Bites, Dark Duets: Musical Mayhem* by Michael McCarty, *Little Creatures* by Michael McCarty, *A Little*

Help from My Fiends by Michael McCarty, *A Hell of a Job* by Michael McCarty, *Laughing in the Dark* by Michael McCarty, *Attack of the Two-Headed Poetry Monster* by Mark McLaughlin & Michael McCarty, *Revenge of the Two-Headed Poetry Monster* by Michael McCarty & Mark McLaughlin, and *Fear & Desire* by S.A. Gambino & Michael McCarty.

TERRIE LEIGH RELF lives in San Diego, California, and has been a writer, editor, and writing coach for a variety of independent presses over the decades. To date, she has over 1,000 publishing credits that include non-fiction, fiction, and poetry, and is the author of such books as: *Letting Out the Demons, Sisterhood of the Blood Moon, Postcards from Space, The Waters of Nyr, Networking Tips for Writers: Envisioning Success, The Intergalactic Cookbook* (with Marge Simon & Sandy DeLuca), and *The Blood Journey* series: *The Blood Journey, Book I* and *The Blood Journey Saga, Book II: The Ancient One,* both of which were co-authored with Henry Lewis Sanders.

C.L. SHERWOOD hails from Deep East Texas and leads a triple life—one as an educator, teaching English and literature to the world's next generation of college-goers and future writers; another as a freelance writer and editor; and lastly as a darkly and somewhat depraved horror writer whose supernatural short stories have appeared in publications such as *Eldritch Tales* and *Mangled Matters* online and *Dark Cities: Dark Tales* by Michael McCarty.

HOLLY A. ZALDIVAR lives in the Lone Star State and is an English Professor—Adjunct Faculty, Northwest Vista Community College. In her spare time, she is the pet mother and is the beta reader for many horror authors.

And be sure to check out…

Lake Livingston: August, 1961

Mark Gaitlin is 15, the son of one of the wealthiest men in Texas, and on the most boring summer vacation of his life. His days are filled with the pomp and circumstance of country club life, while his nights are a parade of one embarrassment after another at the hands of giggling teenage girls.

But the piney woods above Lake Livingston are dark at night, and they hold many secrets for an impressionable youngster on the cusp of becoming a man. And one night, after skinny dipping in the lake with a mysterious local girl, Mark Gaitlin's life takes a crazy turn into the fire and brimstone religion of backwoods snake handlers and abandoned villages haunted by old family secrets. If he can survive the snakes and the ghosts and his own family's dark history, he just might make it out of the woods alive.

And something else…he just might become a man.

www.ingramcontent.com/pod-product-compliance
Lightning Source LLC
Chambersburg PA
CBHW070954190726
48292CB00004B/1454